Donut Shop Lovers

Donut Shop Lovers
short fiction by
Melissa Steele

TURNSTONE PRESS

Copyright © 1999 Melissa Steele

Turnstone Press
607 – 100 Arthur Street
Artspace Building
Winnipeg, Manitoba
Canada R3B 1H3
www.TurnstonePress.com

All rights reserved. No part of this book may be reproduced or transmitted in any form or by any means—graphic, electronic or mechanical—without the prior written permission of the publisher. Any request to photocopy any part of this book shall be directed in writing to the Canadian Copyright Licensing Agency, Toronto.

Turnstone Press gratefully acknowledges the assistance of the Canada Council for the Arts, the Manitoba Arts Council and the Government of Canada through the Book Publishing Industry Development Program for our publishing activities.

The quote on pages 101–102 is from *Selected Poems* by Mark Strand.
Copyright © 1979, 1980 by Mark Strand.
Reprinted by permission of Alfred A. Knopf Inc.
The quote on page 131 is from "The Rewaking" by William Carlos William, from *Collected Poems 1939–1962, Volume II.*
Copyright © 1953 by William Carlos Williams.
Reprinted by permission of New Directions Publishing Corp.

Original cover art by Michelle Yates

Design: Manuela Dias

Printed and bound in Canada by
Friesens for Turnstone Press.

Canadian Cataloguing in Publication Data

Steele, Melissa, 1963–

Donut shop lovers

Short Stories.
ISBN 0-88801-238-1

I. Title.

PS8587.T342 D65 1999   C813'.54   C99-920178-6
PR9199.3.S7812 D65 1999

For George
because everything is.

Table of Contents

LATERAL MOVES
UNCONNECTED STORIES
Sorry, Old Boy   /3
Get Back   /15
Make Me   /27
Emergencies   /37
Jane   /45
Donut Shop Lovers   /57
You have to Wait Till Valentine's Day   /65
Lateral Moves   /81

STAINED LEATHER & OTHER ACTS OF GOD
CONNECTED STORIES
Like Blown Glass   /85
More, Mommy, More   /97
Lint Picking   /109
Sookie Rat   /115
Arrivals   /123
But Not Yet   /131

LATERAL MOVES

Sorry, Old Boy

For Jeannie's fourth birthday party, we invited some neighbourhood kids and hired a clown. The clown was Jimmy's idea. Laura, the clown, was pretty good with balloon animals and silly voices, and only a few of the kids were afraid of her. Jeannie was a really gracious host, the queen of the day: "Welcome to Jeannie Marnie Anderson's fourth birthday celebration. Presents go right here on the kitchen table. Come and join the others in the yard. There is a clown here for your pleasure." The party went by, the way little-kid parties do. The kids were giddy until Jeannie opened her presents. Then they fought over the Bendable Barbie, got sick of the clown and found some sandbox toys to squabble over. Jimmy took a picture of Jeannie and the clown feeding each other birthday cake, and then it was time for the kids to go. While I was cleaning up, Jimmy drove the clown home. He staggered in around three in the morning.

I was sweet to him. I didn't ask him if he thought the clown came, because I didn't care. I'd already planned our escape.

I FELT BAD about things not working out between Jimmy and me, but I got Jeannie out of the bargain and that made it worthwhile. She's such a smart kid. When she was two, she could sing the whole alphabet. When she was four, she could already write her name and read a bit. A few days after the party, I took her out for ice cream at the Dutch Maid Ice Cream Parlour. I wanted to explain things to her.

"Your daddy still loves you, but he's got a wandering dick. We can't have that in our family."

Jeannie barely flinched. "Order me a child-sized chocolate-vanilla twist, Mama," she commanded in her bird voice.

"Today is a special day. You can have the grown-up size."

"Even if I can't finish it?"

"Even if."

"Are we celebrating the wandering dick?"

"Yeah, we're celebrating."

What a kid. When I got the cones, she wanted me to tell her a story about "the amazing adventures of Mama and Jeannie against the big bad world." We always told big-bad-world adventure stories, but this time I just told her what a special little girl she was. I told her that all her dreams would come true because she was so loved. I knew I should have said again that her daddy loved her too, but the words just stuck like a lump and wouldn't come out. I remember how my mother had always referred to my dad as "Dad" or "Andy" when they were still together, but after they'd split up, he became "your father" or "their father," depending on her audience. The difference isn't subtle. "Ask Dad" says, "Our family is a seamless zone of love and nurturing"; "Ask your father" says, "How could I have been so stupid as to have a child with that no-good bastard?" But right now it seemed like a bad omen to say Jimmy's name and like a lie to call him Dad. He wasn't much of a dad, after all. Of course, Jeannie understood instinctively and didn't ask annoying questions like,

"When is Daddy coming home?" or, "What do I tell Monica when she wants Daddy to give us a double-decker piggy-back ride?"

We sat at the counter for a while, licking our cones and watching other parents negotiating with their kids over ice cream: a mother with four kids under six in tow snarling, "Absolutely no special toppings, no dips, no nuts, no cherries and no whining"; a father on visitation day saying, "Have whatever you want, honey," to a scowling, overweight ten-year-old dressed in khaki.

Jeannie took my thumb in her hand and gave it a gentle pull. "Let's go, Mama. Let's go walking."

We took what was left of our cones and made our way to the riverbank. The sun was too hot and too heavy in the sky. The city was buzzing with sounds of cyclists and car radios. People in spandex jock gear and black sunglasses were smoking and tanning anonymously along the riverbank, lulled into peacefulness by the heat. It was hard to imagine that everything might not be fine. I looked over at Jeannie, and she had a clown mouth of ice cream on most of her face. What wasn't on her face was melting around her little fist. I looked again and saw she was crying, a silent, elegant, little-girl cry.

"Don't be sad, sweetie," I said deliberately and without any edginess. "If you're sad, I just might burst." I meant to be comforting, but I only got her crying harder.

"I, I can't finish it," she sobbed, holding up the dripping cone. "I can't, I'm too full. I can't."

"Damn it, honey, just throw it away. Throw it away, for Christ's sake." I hissed loud enough for a few tanners to turn their blank faces in our direction. But Jeannie just stood there with ice cream oozing through her upheld, defiant little fist. She was of a generation that believed littering was a mortal sin. When I was growing up, "the environment" meant green grass, asphalt, gum wrappers and cigarette butts. The world was our ashtray; sidewalks and parking lots were our "orbits." But Jeannie was frozen to the spot, unable to discard the sticky mess before it got worse. I took her by her free arm and dragged her stiff little body home, dripping and oozing the rest of the ice cream on the path along the way.

At home, we took a just-warm bath, which calmed us both down. Then Jeannie put on one of my big T-shirts, and I put on one of Jimmy's. We climbed into the rollicking waterbed and set the thermostat to a comfortable 75 degrees F. I read her stories until she got bored with that and started reading to me. She read me almost all of *Hop on Pop* and part of *The Cat in the Hat*. Listening to her precise little voice, it seemed like I really didn't care about Jimmy and the clown-lady and I stopped hating myself for losing it over a ruined ice cream cone. After a while, Jeannie wanted to play "Rock-a-Bye Baby," so I bounced up and down on the edge of the bed to make waves and sang until she fell asleep. She was a hard-core sleeper, someone who took sleeping seriously. She always slept with her fists clenched and her knees tucked up almost to her chin. I snuggled in beside her and thought about how I was going to make everything up to her—how her life was going to be full and balanced and glazed by love from this day on. I thought about how having a kid makes you strong, not because you have to be, but because however you've fucked up and been fucked over, the kid is just beginning and there's still hope for her. For Jeannie, I didn't just feel hope; it was more like absolute certainty.

I read once that children grow in bursts or spurts like muffin batter in a hot oven. Watching Jeannie, it seemed like if I looked hard enough, I could see her growing bigger and wiser. I watched her eyes flutter under their lids and felt her imagination forming right there in front of me. All at once I understood that we had no time to lose.

THE NEXT MORNING, Jeannie and I put our suitcases on the platform and got on the Greyhound bus going east. We could have taken the one going west, but the eastbound bus left forty-five minutes earlier. Jeannie was excited and refused to take off her sunglasses or let me take off mine, even though the bus had tinted windows and it was cloudy outside. I told Mama-and-Jeannie stories for almost three hours, all the way to Kenora where we stopped for lunch at the downtown depot. I ordered us a hamburger each and a large fries to share and told her to eat up because I had a surprise for her. I went over to the waitress and whispered in her ear. After she cleared our plates, she brought Jeannie a piece of red velvet cake, the kind that is almost blood red, with five candles stuck on it. The waitress and I sang "Happy Birthday" to Jeannie, and then she made her wish and blew out the candles. "Happy birthday, sweetheart," I told her, and the waitress smiled and dabbed her eyes. "Five years old," she said, as if the age itself were some kind of superhuman achievement.

If Jeannie was surprised at having her fifth birthday party in a bus depot, only a few days after she had turned four, she did not let on. For presents, I let her pump eight quarters into her choice of those cheap-plastic-toy-and-candy machines that proliferate in depots and airports. She got a Sailor Moon tattoo, two candy necklaces, and a tiny yellow squirt gun. She was the luckiest five-year-old in the world.

Jeannie slept most of the way to Thunder Bay. As we pulled into the depot, I shook her gently to wake her up and told her to "act natural." She put her sunglasses back on and sucked the candies from her necklace while we collected our things. It was about 8:30 and just twilight. We quickly made our way north, away from the bus depot and the lake, towards Olive Street, where the depot security guard had told me we could find a place to stay. Thunder Bay felt like Winnipeg except the trees were greener and there were hills. It was wetter; the air smelled like fresh water and only a bit like fish because of Lake Superior.

We passed a fire hall where the firemen were out playing volleyball in the parking lot. A couple of them waved at Jeannie, and she said, "Hi!" They all looked like strapping good husbands and fathers—strong, healthy, relaxed and poised to save the innocent from harm on a moment's notice. We didn't look lost or out of place, so none of them offered to come to our rescue.

Though it was early September, it was a hot evening, and I started to feel frustrated as we walked along, passing houses and people who had comfortable, secure lives. Nobody looked twice at us. Jeannie held my hand as if she were certain that I could take care of her no matter what. She wasn't tired because she'd slept so much on the bus, but she seemed almost bored. I wanted her to say, "Mama, where are you taking me? Mama, what are you doing?" Instead she readjusted her Sailor Moon backpack while she chewed on the string that was left over from her candy necklace. She looked dully around, and her feet went pat, pat, pat next to mine.

"Just where do you think we're going, birthday girl?"

"An adventure. We're going somewhere super special. Is it a surprise, Mama?"

"It sure is."

Luckily, we only had to stay at the shelter for a few days before we were hired as live-in help for Karen Feiffer and her family. The Olive Street Home for Women and Children was called "the shelter" by everyone there because while the place provided shelter, it did not provide anything resembling "home." Jeannie wondered why the furniture was nailed to the floor and the mattresses Krazy-glued to their frames. She asked each staff member, but none of them knew.

One of the other residents, a woman mottled with bruises and dressed completely in various neon shades, offered, "so we don't mainline 'em. You could get quite a high on mattress dust, little princess."

Jeannie moved closer to me. She wrinkled her nose, but didn't say anything. The neon junkie's daughter was about Jeannie's age, but she had a screeching quality to her voice and she complained and bullied non-stop: "This place smells like piss." "These toys suck." "I don't hafta listen to you." "My Daddy's gonna cut off yer ear if you don't shuddup." Jeannie and I stayed out most of the days and only came back to the shelter to sleep.

KAREN AND DANIEL FEIFFER had five kids and one of those big old houses with sloping floors and porches everywhere that are made for kids to grow up in. Daniel was a firefighter and Karen had been an archaeologist. Daniel had that quiet authority that dads in old movies have. When he had time to spend with his children, he either roughhoused or taught them first aid and emergency response. At dinner, he gave them pop safety quizzes. "You are walking home from school when a stranger beckons you to his car. He says he needs directions. What do you do?" After dinner he chased them around and pretended to be a tiger.

Karen was beautiful and goddess central in the house. She'd been in a bus accident two years before, during a dig in India. She was paralyzed from the waist down. She also had a form of memory loss that made her repeat little phrases over and over. Sometimes she communicated normally, but mostly she sat in her chair and said, "Sorry, old boy," over and over, the way parrots say "Polly want a cracker." We had never talked about her prognosis, but I assumed it was bleak, or at best mysterious.

My job was to look after Karen and the kids and manage the house. Jeannie's job was to go to kindergarten with Andrea, the youngest little girl. I liked the early mornings the best. I would put out the cereal boxes and make a pitcher of orange juice and batches and batches of cinnamon toast. Davie and Julie, the two oldest kids, took the younger ones to school, and I cleaned up the dishes and then sat with Karen and helped her with whatever she needed to do. Some days she couldn't or wouldn't ask for anything, but most days she would say, "Sorry, old boy, my hair—it's time for a wash." She would wheel herself over to the sink and lay her head back. Her hair was long and yellow, with auburn streaks. I would wrap it around my fist to keep it from disappearing down the drain. Afterwards, we sat on the porch and drank Ruby Mist tea while I combed out her hair and braided it. She liked it wound up in a tight spiral and piled high on her head in a schoolmarmish way that detracted from the painfully readable quality of her face. If she was lucid, she might tell me stories of the dig in Canmore, Alberta, where she had met Daniel when they were both twenty years old. Love is inevitable when you are digging up dinosaur fossils side by side under a naked northern summer sky; that was how she explained it. She also liked to talk about the children and the clever and amusing things they had said and done.

At 11:30, I left her for the ten minutes it took to go and pick up Jeannie and Andrea from kindergarten. Andrea used her skipping rope to tie her ankle to Jeannie's, and they walked home as Siamese twins joined at the socks. They spent the afternoon in the garden, playing jungle queens and tying up various stuffed-animal predators. When the older kids got home from school, I left Davie in charge and went to do the marketing. It was easy to cook for so many—I made big vats of chili or spaghetti or stews and sturdy whole-grain breads. My hands smelled like yeast, and the fine wisps of hair around my face were dusted with flour. It was like we were all at summer camp. Everyone, even Jeannie, had a good appetite and asked for seconds most nights.

Daniel worked a lot. He was often called away on an

emergency in the middle of a meal or halfway through a game of tiger, or before he could finish instructing Davie on the fine points of CPR. He disappeared and reappeared in the house so often and so swiftly that none of us paid much attention to his absences. When he was home, there was an extra-tingly, night-before-Christmas feeling, and the kids got a little louder and sillier, hoping for a nod or a pat on the head from him. Jeannie took to him right away, and called him "The Dad," though the other kids called him silly things like "Danny Bananny" or, when they hadn't seen him for a long time, "Whozit," to which he would respond, "You're it!" and start tickling or, if the kid was small enough, like Jeannie or Andrea, swing her through the porch by her heels.

When Daniel was home, Karen would relax and let some of her grief loose. She knew she was safe and loved, and gave up a little on her effort to talk coherently. Her "Sorry, old boy" came out in a whispering chant, like a spell or an ancient prayer. Her voice was the echo of a faraway drum; Daniel and the kids' laughter and squeals made up the melody. After he had been home for a while she would get tired, and Daniel would carry her up the stairs and we would put her to bed. The kids would all come in and kiss her goodnight, even Jeannie, and then they would whirl Daniel off for more play and instructions. I would stay with Karen and read to her if she was up for it, or listen to her talk until she fell asleep.

When everyone else was asleep, sometimes Daniel and I would sit on the porch and talk. He was the kind of person who treated everyone the same. "It goes with the job," he said. "You don't stop to ask about somebody's past or to see into their mortal soul before you pull them out of a burning building." I wanted to tell him about my past, my burnt-out buildings and who I was. I wanted him to single me out and say, "Ardyth, you are like no one else. Thank God I met you. You have made me alive again." But if he had said those things, he would have been coming on to me, and he would have shattered everything I needed to believe about the Feiffers. I needed the Feiffers to be a happy, healthy family, something that couldn't be threatened by simple, boring human interferences like sex or other people.

Jeannie and I lived with the Feiffers for three blessed, perfect months. We were truly made part of a family. But gradually, I started to notice that Karen was getting better. Her speech was clearer, she repeated herself less and seemed more aware of what was happening. One morning, she reminded me to add peanut butter to the shopping list and that Julie had an orthodontist appointment.

"Don't you have a fine memory for details all of a sudden," I said.

"Sorry, old boy. Sorry, sorry old boy," she said, and then we both laughed.

"I'm really getting better, aren't I?" she said. We looked at each other and our eyes filled up with tears. We seemed to be part of a miracle. I leaned over to hug her, but my embrace was stiff and brief. I knew then that Karen would find a way to get her life back and that Jeannie and I could not be part of that. We would cease to be useful. I felt like Pinocchio would have felt if, after getting back home with Geppetto, after all his adventures and the happy ending, he'd woke up a wooden boy again; like the velveteen rabbit summarily returned to sawdust after having been made real.

I pulled away, but kept my hands on her shoulders. "Let's be cautiously optimistic," I said.

"I've always been cautiously optimistic," she said, and smiled at me. There was a new something shining in her eyes. It was a mischievous something, hopefulness I guess, or maybe she just wasn't so tired. I half-expected her to leap out of her chair and teach me some dance steps. Suddenly, I was thinking about Jimmy again, how people give you everything and then just take it away again. How having something good is only a breath away from losing it.

"Why don't you take the afternoon off?" Karen suggested, and I had to turn my face away, afraid of what it would show. "I can handle Jeannie and Andrea for a few hours."

"I don't know, Karen. Don't you have to take this slow?"

"I am. I have. I will. Trust me with our little girls for the afternoon. I've had to lean on you so much."

IT WAS EASY to find Daniel. He wasn't at the fire station, but on duty at the game reserve, where city firefighters were patrolling to prevent flare-ups of a recently extinguished blaze. I paged him, and he met me at the coffee shop of the Thundering Giant motel, just off Highway One. He seemed smaller without his worshipful swarm of children. He was a king in his castle, but at highway motels there are no kings—only desperate, tired people who belong somewhere else.

"Everything all right at home?" he asked in his ready-for-action firefighter voice.

I was afraid he would judge me irresponsible—neglectful in my duties. "Karen's got the two girls. She wanted to be left with them. She thought she could handle it."

His face relaxed and his voice was kind. "So, what gives?"

"Me." I started to cry. "I give and I give and there's nothing left."

"You're not happy with us?" He pushed my bangs out of my eyes like you would for a child and started to laugh at me. "We'll make you happy. Whatever it takes."

Flirting is horrid, soul-mucking work. To do it well, you have to be poised to fool your companion and yourself. You have no overt designs, no specific plans and no hopes. Every word must convey the possibility of retreat and conquest. The "I'm so sensitive and pathetic" stuff worked on Daniel like gasoline on a forest fire. It was easy to pull off, because it was true, and Daniel practically leaped to the rescue. It was disappointing. I was expecting him to at least need to get drunk first. I'd been hoping for a few moments of agonizing moral conflict in his handsome, wise face before he slipped his arm around my waist and helped me to the front desk, where we got the afternoon rate on a room.

Daniel was good at everything, even making love to his babysitter on his coffee break. He didn't rush and he didn't ask me if I was "okay," not even once. He was deliberate about it, and only a little bit sad. He undressed me with his fingers and his teeth and then picked me up as effortlessly as an ant carries a crumb, and centred me exactly on the bed. I made an effort to turn over—Jimmy always liked to try unconventional angles. But Daniel held me facing him. There was nothing trendy or circus-like about his lovemaking. He made it clear that he didn't want anything from me by way of performance or reassurance. I was the instrument, he was the musician. Since I couldn't reach his mouth, I turned my head and sucked on the hairs on his forearm. He must have been coated in bug spray from his stint in the woods. He tasted like poison; my tongue and my lips started to tingle and then went completely numb. I wanted to say something, just to see if I could still talk.

"Daniel?"

Sex is supposed to make you vulnerable; it is supposed to change you; it is a metaphor for giving away part of yourself. But Daniel never lost his "all in a day's work" attitude. I could hear him telling Davie, "When you set out to do something, son, you give it your best. Never less than your best."

"Daniel?"

"Concentrate, Ardyth. Just concentrate. That-a-girl."

JEANNIE AND I took the night bus home. I told her it would be easier to leave at night, easier not to say goodbye. I told her everybody makes mistakes, even mommies.

"When I grow up, I'm going to be Jeannie Feiffer and I'm going to be a Fire Lady Fighter and Andrea's going to be my sister and I will live in a house with a garden."

"Your daddy's going to be so happy to see you. He misses you so much. He can't wait to see his big girl."

"Will we come back and stay with the Feiffers?"

"Tomorrow is so special, because you never know what you might do."

"Now I'll always be a little bit sad and a little bit happy. When I'm home with Daddy, I'll miss Andrea and the Feiffers, and when I'm with them, I'll miss home and how things were before."

I couldn't bear for Jeannie to be sad. I told her what a special girl she was. I told her that because she was so special, something magic had happened to her. All this time she thought she was five years old, in kindergarten and living in Thunder Bay, was really like a dream. When we got to Dryden in a few hours, we would have a little un-party for her, and she could be four again for the rest of the year. When we got home, it would be as if we had never been away. Next year she could start kindergarten with Monica and all her friends at home.

"I don't want to be four. Can I turn seven?"

"Four is an even number, honey. You can multiply and divide it. I'll teach you later. Now go to sleep."

Riding in a bus across the Trans-Canada Highway in the middle of the night is a kind of anaesthetic. Inside the cocoon of metal and glass and blue-and-gold-striped upholstery there is no sense of distance or forward motion, only the even drone of the motor and the inevitable wheezy rustling of strangers. You can barely see out the tinted windows and what you do see is indistinguishable from one hour to the next. I thought I would tell Jeannie sometime when she was old enough to understand that when you go very far and very fast, it often feels like you are standing still.

It was close to three in the morning when the bus began to slow down and work its way into the town of Dryden. The town was deeply stagnant, undisturbed by our arrival, but Jeannie felt the bus lurch and heave in its lower gears as we approached the Dryden depot. The irregular movement woke her, and she sat up, rubbed her eyes and looked around.

The driver announced a half-hour "rest stop" in Dryden, but most of the passengers stayed in their seats. I took my little daughter's hand and led her off the bus and into the grunge-encrusted terminal.

Bus stations always smell like piss and dirty socks. They are forever occupied by the wayward and the unlucky, but in the middle of the night, the inhabitants are particularly desperate and disconnected. The Dryden depot was empty except for one family—a bald, rumpled father, a mucus-and-jam-faced toddler and a skinny eleven-year-old girl in a tiny polka-dot dress. They hunched together on a turquoise plastic bench, not moving, except for the girl, who tugged rhythmically at the hem of her dress. Under the throbbing fluorescent light, even the toddler looked ancient and humourless.

"Can I have my party now? Is it time for my birthday now?"

"Yes, sweet pea. Come and sit in the cafeteria. After you make a wish and blow out the candles, you'll be four years old, but you can dream about turning seven whenever you close your eyes."

"I want red velvet cake. I'll eat it all."

"Me too. Come on. Let's eat."

Get Back

My best friend Ariel was in love with a charismatic animal-rights activist who had undergone three rounds of chemotherapy. She met him at a sit-in protesting the treatment of pregnant mares whose urine is used for human pregnancy tests. The horses are kept pregnant and standing in four-by-six stalls to facilitate the pee collection. Not much of a life.

Ariel is the kind of person who is all principle—no grey areas, no moral crises. She and Ethan had been happily married for fifteen years before she met Greg. She was a good wife and mother and always active in underdog political causes. For her, fidelity went beyond self-control—it was a fact like breathing or aging. I admired Ariel because she wasn't afraid of what she knew.

Once I took her to visit my grandmother when my grandfather was weakening in hospital with only a few days left to live. My grandmother, who had that regal quality very tiny, very old women sometimes have, tottered around her kitchen making tea and fetching soda crackers and dusty lemon drops for us.

As Granny set out the teacups, she started to cry a little. "We had such a good life," she said. "He was always so healthy. I just never thought this would happen to us."

Ariel was a compulsive straight-shooter. She said, in her kind, but matter-of-fact voice, "Mrs. Haley, he's eighty-two years old. His parents are dead. All his brothers and sisters are dead. How could he not die too? What makes him different from everybody else?"

Granny poured the tea and quickly composed herself. "Don't listen to me, dear. Tell me all about your little girl, Ariel. Teresa tells me you had a baby girl."

"Anna is a bright, sturdy little girl who thinks the whole world belongs to her. She's wonderful," Ariel said.

We all laughed and felt more comfortable. Children are a kind of equalizer among mothers and grandmothers. We all hold their very existence in a certain amount of awe.

It was not long after that visit with my grandmother that Ariel fell for Greg. When she told me about him, she talked in the absolute terms of the recently converted. "Greg is not like anyone else. It's not only that he's lived through so much. It's not just that he's, I think, the most truly principled person I've ever met. But he knows me. Really me. What there is between us is the only truth I've ever fully known. I'm so happy. I'm so terrified."

I didn't ask her the difficult questions: Have you told Ethan and Anna yet? What if Greg dies? Has Greg ever had sex? Could he? (Greg was in a wheelchair because of a car accident he was in when he was twelve.) I said, "What are you going to do, Ariel?"

I have to admit, a part of me felt smug, gleeful even, that Ariel was finally in a situation where she might, for once, fail to do the obvious and right thing. What good is it to be only human unless everyone else is too?

Ariel said, "This isn't about what I am going to do. I'm doing it. Greg and I have almost three hundred names on our sign-up sheet. Enough to launch the first Canadian chapter of Humans and Animals against Human Abuse of

Animals. How can we not work together? Greg and I are making the world an ever-so-slightly gentler place. How can we not do that together?"

"You're truly amazing, Ariel."

A few days later, I went over to Ariel's to watch Anna for her while she went to another meeting. Anna and I built a playdough bear, and then I showed her it could be fun to clean up toys. She is only two and a half, but Ariel has already taught her to sing "I'm Stickin' with the Union," and she can pretty well count to twenty.

I kept Anna up until late in the afternoon so she would be sleeping when Ariel got home. I knew Ariel would need to debrief. She was only a few minutes late, and we had time to talk before Ethan got home.

"Greg and I are going to facilitate a 'know your animal's rights' workshop next weekend. We're going to have a translator and handouts, and it's going to be great."

"Ariel, are you losing weight?"

"I'm just going twenty-four hours a day. And there's Anna and I have no idea what to make for supper."

"Just make tuna casserole. Men love that. Ethan's got to like it."

"Yeah. Thanks, Teresa. Thanks for looking after Anna and me."

When she said that I felt all right inside. I was looking out for them. I was a good person and a good friend. I wondered if she would have done the same for me. Sure she would, but then I would never ask. Of the two of us, Ariel had always been the one who was in the limelight. My life was more or less uneventful. My husband, Al, was a bum and a drunk, but I'd known that when I married him. I had the kids trained to stay out of his way, and I did the same. My life was manageable. I could be there for Ariel and I would.

Anna woke up early from her nap, and Ariel brought her downstairs. She held her on her lap with a bottle of juice and her blanket. Anna had that quiet, mucusy stare children get after naps. I guaged that we could talk in front of her—she was too dazed to pick up much.

"So how are things with you and Ethan?"

"He can't stop picking on me. Every little thing."

"As if you don't have enough to deal with as it is."

"That's what Greg says. He says never put up with what you can't stand. He has a real spiritual side. Ethan's so 'How much is that? When are you getting home? Do you mind if I turn the game on now?' "

"Ethan's such a guy." I didn't want to say too much. I didn't want to run Ethan down. I've known him almost as long as Ariel, and he's a good guy in his way, but Ariel was really the type who needed something more.

"With Greg, you know, we laugh together. We're a team. You know, we built this protest movement together. What I say matters to him. We complement each other. We connect. Anyway, you'll meet him. You'll see for yourself."

I had to get home to make supper for Al and the kids. It was Thursday, which meant Al would probably go straight to the club after work and probably wouldn't stagger home until eight or nine o'clock. On Thursdays, I always made something Al really liked—Swedish meatballs or gnocchi—just to shame him whenever he did stumble through the door. That night, I planned to feed the kids and get them settled with their homework and then call Ariel again, just to see how she was doing. I know she is a grown-up and doesn't need me to take care of her, but I couldn't stop thinking about what it must be like to finally find love after fifteen years of relative peace with someone else. It seemed like a pretty bad joke on her, and I wanted to make it easier for her if I could.

I HAD TO WORK days the rest of the week, and didn't see Ariel except for one lunch hour, when I saw her at the Humans and Animals against Human Abuse of Animals (HAHAA) meeting. They were a pretty wild bunch—one woman came dressed as a pink faux-fur leopard, and another one, a guy named Jesus, came in a tan bodystocking, representing a naked fox, I suppose. Greg called the meeting to order and got everyone's attention by reading out the statement he and Ariel had written about the pregnant mares: "In four-by-six stalls, mothers-to-be stand catheterized, bored and sometimes with untended open sores. Their pain is in their eyes." I understood instantly what Ariel saw in Greg. He had been a really powerful wheelchair athlete in high school—he'd even made the provincial wheelchair basketball team—and though he had been ravaged by the cancer and the chemo, you could still see the grace and definition in his shoulders. His hair had fallen out and he wore a knitted Peruvian cap, like a little rainbow yarmulke, and his eyes were like cat's eyes— glowing with too much colour; there was no room for whites in his eyes. He talked about how the next protest had to be something more than just a flashback to the sixties; how the media was sophisticated now; how everything, even whether he got into Heaven or not, would all be a matter of how the story played for the media. Everyone in the room was under the spell of his passionate, compassionate, reasonable voice. I knew what he and Ariel saw in each other: they were alike in their ability to see and say exactly what was important.

I had to go back to work after the meeting, but I hung around outside watching Ariel and Greg as they left. She held the car door for him and he eased himself into the passenger seat. She handled his wheelchair with the same nonchalant familiarity that she had when she closed up Anna's stroller and popped it into the trunk. They drove off, and I felt a little envious of Ariel having Greg there beside her in the sealed compartment of her car. When I was in high school and practising for my driver's test, I'd had a mad crush on my science teacher, Mr. Filbun. I had no real interest in having a driver's licence, except that every day when I saw Mr. Filbun waiting for the bus after school, I had a fantasy about coming around the corner in my father's 1971 Dodge Dart (white with a red-leather interior), pulling up beside the bus stop, and asking, "Would you like a ride somewhere, Mr. Filbun?" I could imagine him sliding in beside me on the bench seat and I could hear the heavy door slamming shut, but I couldn't see the details of the fantasy past that point. It seemed that once I had him in the private, intimate space inside my dad's car, everything else would just naturally follow.

I never did have the guts to invite Mr. Filbun for a ride, though I did get my licence that year. Anyway, Al asked me if I'd "be willun to go to the grad with him, if there wasn't nobody else you was sweet on or nuthin," as he put it. Mr. Filbun wasn't exactly "nobody else or nuthin," so I went with Al. He got hammered before the dance even started, and we spent the night drag racing up and down Pembina Highway. When the kids asked me why I married their father, I would say, "I got taken for a ride."

I felt quite an ache all afternoon at work, thinking about Ariel and Greg and about what it must be like to be in love with someone you admired and adored and who loved you back.

Ariel phoned me that night.

"Teresa, he proposed to me. He wants me to leave Ethan and move in with him."

"Oh, Ariel," was all I could muster as a reply.

Ariel started crying softly, but didn't let her emotions erupt.

"It's okay, just cry it out," I said. I figured she had a right to be sad about some things even though she was about to have the kind of happiness most people just read about in books. "Does Ethan know yet?"

"You don't understand," she said. "I told Greg no. I told him I couldn't leave Ethan. That I couldn't do that to Anna. I told him you don't just walk away from a marriage after fifteen years. I talked to Ethan and he's furious and hurt, but we're going to get some counselling. Thank God I didn't let this thing go too far."

I couldn't believe what I was hearing. "Are you sure, Ariel? Are you really sure? Because real love isn't something everyone gets a chance at. Some people never even sniff at anything like what you and Greg could be together." I tried to swallow the rage that was building in me. I had always looked up to Ariel. I couldn't understand how she could just toy with Greg and then toss him in the bin when the game got serious.

"Teresa, I've thought this through. My feelings for Greg are strong, but they are just that—feelings. They aren't fifteen years and a child. I'm just afraid because what if I can't get over it and what if things are never the same between me and Ethan? What if I've wrecked everything?"

I wanted to say, "Wouldn't that serve you right, little missy? Wouldn't that be your just desserts?" but I held back. She was suffering. She was scared. She was confused. Maybe she would see in time that there was no going back to the way things were. "What did Greg say?" I asked her.

"He said he needs me. He said that if he wasn't a cripple at death's door, he thought I wouldn't hesitate to be with him. And then he started to cry and said I have to love him. He said I want to torture him because I want to punish him for having cancer. He didn't come right out and say that if I didn't leave Ethan, he would literally just curl up and die, but pretty close."

"And?"

"And I think that's manipulative bullshit. I know he's scared. And I feel for him, but I resent that he wants to make me his keeper."

I wanted to say, "Don't you think that's pretty selfish, Ariel? Isn't Greg just a little bit right that you are scared to go with him down the road he's on?" but instead I said something trite and hollow like, "Cool heads will prevail come morning time," and suggested we could all use a good night's sleep.

AFTER THAT ARIEL and I kept our distance. She didn't call me up in the middle of the night to tell me the latest, and I was more glad than sorry. I kept going to the HAHAA meetings. Ariel did too for a while, but she kept things strictly business with Greg. She left right away after the meetings, and I was the one to give Greg a ride. Driving Greg home in my rusty Suburu, we talked animal-rights strategy and he told me more about his fight against cancer. He was planning to go to Mexico for experimental herbal treatments. He said he had no intention of dying without a fight. There he was in the passenger seat beside me—a man who wasn't afraid to speak only the truth; a man who was fully human because he understood the dignity of other creatures and because he was in the midst of his own cockfight with death. Unlike with my science teacher, Mr. Filbun, I had no trouble imagining where such a car ride might lead.

ASKING AL TO LEAVE was about as smooth as wiping a kid's runny nose or cleaning the kitchen counter. Al was miserable and got drunk and cried and carried on. It was pretty much like any other day with Al. He told me he loved me and he didn't deserve me and even that he would quit drinking—all that garbage people say when they're desperate. I think he was grateful in a way for permission to slink off and go and drink himself into oblivion. I think that had been his private ambition for a long time. Maybe always.

Greg and I got married a week after my divorce came through and two weeks after the doctors declared that they could do nothing more for him. The cancer was in his liver and pancreas now, and there was no point in further treatment. We would have raged against the doctors, but we were too much in love to believe them. We left my kids with my sister and went to Mexico for the natural treatment that would save Greg's life. Down there we saw children and animals living like no one should ever have to live. Kids in rags with matchstick legs and moon faces lived on garbage and begging. Starving wild dogs sometimes killed and ate those children when there wasn't enough garbage to go around. We talked a lot about HAHAA and about how we could start a chapter down in Mexico. We even held a meeting, but none of the locals came.

Greg was getting the latest miracle treatment—injections of some kind of beeswax and strange tablets that smelled like kiwi-flavoured seaweed. But he was weaker every day and the pain was often out of control. He said his body felt like it was infested with right-wing counter-revolutionary termites. They navigated through his bloodstream and were rioting through every part of him. On the day we travelled back to Canada, he was so weak and so light that once I got his wheelchair to the plane, I carried him myself to his seat. The last few weeks he seemed to be losing focus and he slept a lot. When he wasn't sleeping, he was moaning. He called for his mother sometimes. Sometimes he called for me. Once or twice I think he called for Ariel, but I wasn't sure.

Everyone—the doctors, his family, his friends, even Al—seemed to think I'd brought him home to die. They were patient with me the way a good teacher is with a child who can't learn, but I heard them whispering from the other room phrases like "getting it over with" and "moving on." But strangely, it never occurred to me that Greg would actually die. Even up until the final seconds of his life, even as he breathed his last breath, I felt sure that divine intervention was imminent. I thought about what Ariel had said to my grandmother when my grandfather was dying: "What makes him different from everybody else?" I knew that there were rules in life, but there must also be exceptions to those rules. Greg had to be the exception; I thought I could love him into full recovery.

The funeral was on one of those bright November days

when you can see your breath and the ground is hard and noisy where you walk even though there isn't any snow yet. Ariel was there with Ethan. She was kind to me, and Ethan kept a polite distance when Ariel and I cried and when we hugged each other. Ariel said that she had thought often about Greg and me and that she wished me well. She said that she and Ethan were on the road back. Neither of us said, "I'll call you" or "Let's get together soon." Then Ethan came up and gave me a hug. "Well, we've left Anna with a sitter. We've got to get back," Ethan said.

"We've really got to get back," Ariel repeated.

I watched Ethan and Ariel get into their car and slam the doors shut. "Get back," I said to nobody in particular. I looked over at the mound of fresh dirt over Greg's coffin. "Get back," I said to the autumn sun and the leaves blowing around the cemetery and the people standing around in that stunned, nervous way people do at funerals. "Get back to your lives everyone." And I looked wildly around for mine.

MAKE ME

ABBIE LIKED READING NOVELS. It didn't matter if they were trashy like Danielle Steel's *Remembrance* or classics like *Wuthering Heights* or *The Red and the Black*. She chose them for their length, not their status. She liked small type and lots of pages. It was distraction. The intensity of the distraction didn't matter. It made her feel adult and happy to climb inside a book that liked the sound of its own voice enough to go on for seven hundred pages or more. She also liked sex, she couldn't get enough, and she hated work and television.

Because she hadn't finished high school, Abbie thought she was stupid. Brian said she wasn't stupid, just whiny. Abbie said she'd rather be stupid, and anyway she was stupid so what did Brian know about it? Brian was sitting at the counter drinking coffee and waiting for Abbie to be finished so he could take her home. She wasn't allowed to start putting things away and do the floors until quarter to eleven, even though she hadn't had a customer since nine o'clock. She was leaning over the dishwasher reading a hardcover book she'd taken from the town library. The book said "Great Literature Series" on the back cover, but it was the usual stuff: love, disappointment, fancy explanations, but nothing simple enough to provide a real moral. Abbie could already tell that the hero would die in the end. He wanted too much, and besides, he was lower class and trying to mix with dukes and counts and even a princess. She was just at the point where it seemed everything was possible for him—everyone liked him, his looks, his cleverness, his shyness. The women were all fighting over him, but she was only on page 300. There were too many pages left for him not to fail, ruin everything, get disillusioned, find God or get married. It wasn't a bad book. At least she didn't want him to fail and didn't think he deserved it. She could feel along with the hero the delirium of possibility, even though as an outsider, she was more sceptical than he could be.

Brian started talking about plans for the addition he wanted to build on their house. It was quarter to eleven, so Abbie started sweeping up. She didn't care about the addition. What Brian really wanted was a baby, probably a whole family, but Abbie wasn't the family type. She'd already been through that against her will once, as a child, and she wasn't about to do it again voluntarily. Thinking about children made it hard for her to breathe. Childhood was like an almost intelligible nightmare. The objects of childhood—parents, school, monkey bars, the lake in the summer—were just slightly too large to be recognizable in her memory. They were like close-ups, made too big and too general to be anything other than monster shapes and monster shadows. The thought of standing back and bringing it all into focus was impossible. It was the same with childhood sounds—the radio, screaming, arguing, laughter—all through a loudspeaker that blurred into a roar of noise. Like nightmares, childhood is something you wake up from and shake off. Abbie was sweeping under the counter and Brian lifted his feet so she could get under his stool. This was a familiar gesture, an adult gesture. It happened every time there was a late-night customer and Abbie closed the café. "Thanks, Brian," she said.

"We could have an extra bedroom in the back, next to the family room," he said. Brian worked with his dad as a building contractor, so he meant business about the addition.

"I want horses," Abbie said. "Why build on that little crummy lot? Let's get a farm."

"When could we afford that? In fifteen years? I'm thirty years old," Brian said.

Abbie was coming by with the mop this time, and Brian lifted his feet. "Thanks." She bent down to pick up a napkin that was balled in the corner of the floor.

"Aw, anyway," Brian said. He looked at her crouched down and thought maybe her skirt was getting too tight. He liked that. She was pretty, but a bit too skinny. He stretched out his leg and nuzzled his foot into the material of her skirt between her legs. "Come on, Abbie. Let's go home."

She stayed crouched a second longer because she was surprised, and she liked to be surprised. "Don't kick me," she said, standing up and coming over to kiss him. He kissed her back, but quickly, because there was a big window and anyone walking by could see in. She wanted to make love that instant, but it was useless asking Brian to do anything out of the ordinary. He had an aversion to getting caught. He had an invisible mother who travelled everywhere with him, telling him, "Think how it would look to other people, Brian." Anyway, she knew tonight would be okay at home.

Abbie and Brian lived in Maberly, a small town about five miles west of Perth, the bigger town where she worked. The road between was gravel and windy. There were little hay farms and dairy farms all along the way. In the car she rolled down the window so she could smell the night and the farms and everyone, even the animals, asleep for the night. She thought, We are both this moment thinking the same identical thought. If we didn't think how it would look to other people, we would stop the car and do it right by the gravel on the side of the highway. It's possible that at this moment, all we want is each other, and we have that. We have everything we want.

"Hey, stupid, roll up your window," Brian said. He was driving and his mind was comfortably in that automatic driver's fog. "It's icing up in here."

Abbie rolled her window all the way down. "It was too hot in here, stupid. You were falling asleep." She leaned over the back seat and unrolled the back window.

"Abbie, cut it out. It's winter. There's frost on the ground. Come on."

"Suffer, stupid. Moron. Illiterate. Hick." She was stretched out over the front seat, unrolling the back window on the driver's side.

"Hey, okay. I didn't mean to call you stupid. I was teasing. Everyone says you're smart. You know I'm crazy about you."

"Freeze your ass. I don't care. See if I care."

"Abbie, don't start going crazy on me. It's boring. Act like an adult for once. I didn't mean anything."

"Imbecile. Ignoramus. Did I forget any? You're not just stupid, you're lazy. It's lucky you can work for your dad. What else could you do?"

Nothing would induce Brian to participate in this level of childishness. Everything she said to him, he knew, was designed to get a reaction. Everything in him refused to react. Brian stopped the car, got out, walked around and rolled up the back windows. When he got back in, Abbie was crying and rolling up her window.

Abbie was used to making scenes like this. They just came out of her the way some people laugh for no reason. It scared her though, because it made her feel so crazy and Brian was so uncrazy. How could he stand her? Maybe he'd tell her to get out of the car and he'd drive away and leave her by the side of the road. She cried and said, "I'm sorry, Brian. I just took it the wrong way. I take everything the wrong way. I'm just tired from work."

Brian hated it when she cried. He wasn't mad. He just wanted to be away from her. Far away. "Forget it," he said. And then they were home.

YOU ARE REALLY ASLEEP and I don't hate you. I hate myself, whining with my voice—do you want to... please, Brian, I just want, I want... whatever you want. Or whining with my hands. Tentative. As if I'm not asking for anything back, as if it's normal, not sexual, to touch you. You patted my shoulder before you went to sleep. That's a different lie. Pat my shoulder like a dog. Whine. You rolled over, hugged yourself and went to sleep. You sleep with your mouth open. You make quick, jerky inhaling sounds—tense, private, selfish sounds. Your knees are bent and your hands, palms together, are pressed between your thighs. Your legs are skinny, the muscles in your thighs always defined. You are really asleep and I don't hate you. The skin on your back is smooth and perfect except for a white triangle scar by one shoulder blade—an arrow, from target-shooting with your brother when you were children. I touch it. It's isosceles. You are oblivious, barely dreaming.

It's not completely dark. There's the neon "Jody's Hardware" sign and some light from the tower in the church across the road. Candlelight and neon. My eyes are used to it and I'm used to you—the shape and shadow of your body sleeping. I squirm and twist and pull at the covers, but nothing affects you. On one elbow, I can lean over and watch the stubble grow, on your face. It only grows at night. That's true. It only grows when you are sleeping, when you can't control it, when you abandon yourself in sleep. Your face is growing darker, the corners of your mouth are uncontrolled, ragged. Your eyelashes are light, and your eyes not looking but easily shut. If you are having a nightmare, it's in your face and not your body. Your face is not an expression. It is indifference, chaotic indifference growing darker. You will shave in the morning. You will look at yourself in the mirror calmly and shave. I could hate you. There is something I hate. It's impossible to sleep. My parents hated each other even though they claimed it had nothing to do with us. Us—me and Alicia, who must have been make-believe; an imaginary twin. I don't remember her, only the pretty name. My parents were great dancers. They took dancing lessons on Thursday nights. They weren't hicks. They moved to the city. My father worked in a bank and combed his hair slick back over his head. They hated each other except for sex. They wanted each other. That's what she told me. Once, in the new house, after Alicia, after I thought she was just pretend, he knocked my mother across the room, against the kitchen counter, and broke her arm. They made love before he took her to the hospital. He carried her upstairs, pulling her panties down. Up, up, up. That's a girl. One step at a time, because they wanted each other so bad. They did it on the landing. She thought it felt like really good shock therapy was supposed to feel. She told me this after, after he was gone for good, so I'd always know what he'd done to her, but she'd wanted him that time. Zap. Zap. Zap. The moral of the story: after, say you didn't mean it.

I can't sleep. I can't sleep. The light is constant: not enough to read by, too much to sleep under. I don't want you any more. I could leave you, go back to Ottawa. There's nothing here. I don't want it. I think about falling from a building. Seven storeys. I would hold my breath, lie on my back in the air and watch the clouds receding. So. I'm not afraid of it. The ground rushing up at me. I would just lie there. It would be instantaneous, the impact, a seven-storey instant impact. Practically forever.

I push all the covers onto you, bury you in the comforter. It's hot. My nightgown is up around my waist. I would like to masturbate to nothing but sensation, think nothing, touch this button, and nothing happens except the button takes over the world. It turns over and explodes slowly, like a slow-motion film of the bomb, like the sun blown up in silence. Fireworks. A firecracker opening on the blackness of space. And opening, and opening... but that doesn't work. I need something human. You are snoring lightly. You would be disgusted if you knew. Horrified. You might even laugh. That almost works, but it's not awful enough. It's boring touching myself; boring shocking you. I am flat on my back, knees bent, right hand moving in circles. Your hand on my throat, lovingly, but too tight. Your face smiling with hatred, your knee between my legs, make me, please. No, that's just awful. Go ahead and hate me. It's boring. My mother didn't get out of bed for almost a year. My wrist hurts—tendonitis. I hold my breath. You and my friend Lesley. You can't help it—she's wearing a white cotton sweatshirt and she's so beautiful. Your hands are pressing her breasts. She doesn't have a face, no Lesley laugh, no Lesley expression, but her nipples are small and red and maybe tender. You don't want to hurt her. You kiss her breasts and suck everywhere, even the hair under her arms and her stomach, even her stomach is perfect. You can't help it, trying to pull down her pants, you don't mean it, but you're so hard your hands are clumsy and you just have to be inside her now, now, but it's too late. You've come all over your trousers and her and you look ridiculous standing there and how am I supposed to feel, spilling over like drink crystals dissolving in warm water?

It's over and I wish it could have been me, but maybe now it's possible to sleep. Her face is available now, and I want to fall asleep holding her. She's smaller than me. I would kiss her eyelids, that's all. You move suddenly in your sleep and say something. I pull my knees up to my chest and my nightgown down around my feet. I like flannel... how it feels....

IN THE DREAM, Alicia and I are little girls. We are wearing pretty pink nightgowns and playing with matches at night on the bathroom floor. There are no grown-ups. We are lighting the matches and throwing them at the drain in the bathtub. Our aim is bad, but the matches are shooting stars and burn up before they land. I am better at it than Alicia. As always, Alicia is better at watching. We are dreadfully excited. One match won't light, and I rub the tip between my fingers till it sparks, but the flint is stuck to my thumb. It doesn't hurt. I hold up my thumb like a candle and make Alicia run her finger through the flame. She's scared, so I tell her it won't hurt, but what doesn't hurt me hurts her. Her nightgown catches on fire and she starts to scream. The material is like plastic or skin, and the flames just dissolve it; lick it away. Instead of helping her, I say, "It's your fault. You shouldn't play with matches." It's my mother's voice, though she isn't in the dream, and it's a muted dream voice that can't reach Alicia or me. Then I am cleaning up. I pile up the burnt-out matches and wipe the bathtub. I wipe the soot from the mirror in circles, but it only smears. The air is thick with chemical smoke, and I will certainly be caught. In a panic I remember Alicia, but the dream doesn't have room for her any more. It's as if she never happened.

"BREATHE, ABBIE," she tells herself, "breathe. You're awake. Stop it."

Brian is a light sleeper in the early morning. He holds her. He comforts her.

"A dream," she says. "A nightmare. A fire. My sister..."

"Abbie, my love," he says. "You're all sweaty." Nothing fazes him. She likes him. His hands are drawing a body for her, tracing it through her nightgown: neck, shoulders, breasts. He is happy. He holds nothing against her. He had been dreaming about flying or something just as good.

They make love from their different corners of the world. It doesn't seem possible to her, the fact of him inside her, of motion, of two together, of Brian and Abbie. His movements aren't violent, but determined. He is trying to get somewhere. Abbie likes surprises, she's always "up for them," but her thoughts are still swirling through the deep crevices of the nightmare and sex is not what she wants at all right now. Her body is still fragile and numb with sleep. He is pushing, pushing, pushing. She closes her eyes and her whole face in a grimace. She is practically awake. He likes his effect on her. The expression on her face is out of control. It is the expression of a woman who has told Brian she loves him, wants to have his child, wants him, Brian, *him*. He believes her as if her passion were something he invented, as if he had the power to make her feel it. There is a point where his faith is coercive. She is no longer aware of distance or doubts. Her body is fully awake and has overcome the confines and terrors of thought. She has lost the faculty of speech. They move together more and more quickly, closing the space, until one of them comes abruptly—another surprise—and they are jarred back into separateness. Brian is holding her wrists tightly and she is smiling at him. She can hardly remember the dream or Lesley.

"Was that good for you, babe?" Brian asks—the usual male ego question.

It *was* good for Abbie, at least the last few minutes, when all the inexpressible feelings—terror, love, rage, hope, hopelessness and joy—were so clearly part of what they were doing to each other.

"You know it. Don't the other girls like you so well?" Abbie says, and pushes his chest to get him to move off of her.

"Only the really dumb ones," he says, giving her nose a sharp little play-bite before pulling away and turning to hug himself back to sleep.

IN THE MORNING, Abbie thought she would stay in bed as long as she could possibly stand it, which didn't turn out to be very long—about forty pages of her book. Brian was gone. He always got up at seven to go to work. She must have been asleep because she didn't remember him getting up today.

Abbie got up, put the kettle on and read in the kitchen while she waited for the water to boil. The characters in her book kept proving their love for each other. They climbed ladders in the middle of the night and offered to sacrifice their own children. Abbie put the book down and got up to make the tea. It was a glaring, sunny day. She didn't start work until four.

EMERGENCIES

NICOL IS SLIDING THE RAZOR across her wrist, keeping it about a millimetre away from her skin. It's just a test run. She is sitting in the bathtub wearing only her pink nylon shorts; gym shorts left over from high school that are ugly but still fit. The plastic sides of the tub are too cool to lean back on, so she is hunched up in the middle with her wrist held up by her knees.

THE APPOINTMENT is at three o'clock.

LENNY IS IN the living room with the pieces of his bicycle spread out on newspaper. Every year he takes the bike apart for spring cleaning. He is meticulous about it, scrubbing down everything from the frame to the tiniest bolt. Nicol knows Lenny won't be finished with the bike in time and will leave the pieces scattered all over the living room.

AT FIRST THEY were just roommates. They started sleeping together when there was a problem with the boiler in the basement. The heat was off and Lenny's sleeping bag loaned out. That was two years ago. They are both still shy with each other, even though they have started to depend on each other and say I love you.

LENNY IS SITTING on the floor staring at the stripped red frame, smoking a joint. He isn't thinking about Nicol or the would-be baby. He is remembering the time when he and his friend Ben broke into the art studio where they both work. They mixed up a batch of poster paints. Ben had wanted to paint rainbows and write, "Let the children play," on the walls. Lenny got carried away. He covered his hands in red paint and did cartwheels across the studio floor. He imagined himself going across the floor, up the wall and then spinning across the ceiling, surrounding the room with a ribbon of red handprints. What happened was that he got halfway across the floor and crashed into some easels. He didn't break them, and his handprints didn't add much to the floor, which already looked like a Jackson Pollock canvas. Ben said, "Hey, forget it. You're such a klutz, Lenny." They dumped the rest of the paint down the sink.

Outside they sat on the steps, freezing cold, sharing a joint. Lenny's hands were still covered in red poster paint, so he did his Baptist minister imitation and washed the Blood of the Lamb from his hands in the snow while solemnly reciting Ben's ancient proverbs from junior high: "The world is your oyster. Grab it by the pearls. Whether you like oysters or not." He kept it up until his fingers were numb and Ben was laughing so hard he was holding his stomach and practically choking.

Lenny would like to reach back into that memory and pick up the easels he'd scattered. He wished he could go back and wipe the floor clean, not just of his handprints, but really clean. Gleaming yellow linoleum. He feels so cluttered he can hardly think. Nicol wouldn't even talk to him today. He was going to tell her that everything would be all right. If she wanted to have the baby, it would be okay. They could get married. He had meant to say, "Why not, Nicol. Let's just go with it," or maybe, "Listen, you know I want whatever you want," but those phrases sound like lines in a script. He tried to imagine himself with a nine-to-five job, probably as a gopher in his dad's office. He would phone her at coffee break to see how the baby was. He would have gone through with it, he was sure, but when he tried to tell her, she just pulled away and looked at him as if she didn't know him, didn't want to know him. The hurt hung on him all day so he couldn't recapture the fantasy about the baby.

NICOL HAS HER fist clenched so the skinny tendons that cut through her wrist protrude slightly. It is a relief she doesn't have ugly blue veins as thick as ropes, like Lenny's. Except for the tautness of the tendons, her wrist is really bland.

The blade barely nicks her skin. It's just like a paper cut. There is a thin line of blood, nothing significant. Her stomach turns over on itself, but it doesn't really hurt.

LENNY GETS UP and pulls the auto switch on the record player. Joan Armatrading starts up again, with no sign of tiring out. "You get too jealous / You rope, you tie me / I need to be free." It's just background. Nicol once asked Lenny how he could listen to the same album over and over again like that, even if it is Armatrading. Lenny just said, "Okay," and put on some la-dee-da jazz record, but then he played that one three times in a row.

Nicol turns the water on to drown out Armatrading, forgetting she is still wearing her shorts. She jumps up, smashing her shoulder on the towel rack. The seat of her shorts is wet and hangs down like soggy diapers. She peels them off and lies down in the tub. The tap is on full blast, but the tub is too big to fill up fast enough for her.

From the hallway Lenny can see most of Nicol in the bathtub. The door to the bathroom has been painted too many times and doesn't close properly. The water is steaming, but she has goosebumps where her skin is exposed. He can't see her face, but imagines it sullen and distant from him. The faceless body doesn't look like it could possibly love him. Her hip bones, breasts and knees jut out. They are hard to look at: wide white patches like hills that once had trees, but have since been logged bare. For an instant he imagines taking the body and caressing it, making it alive, making it respond. In the fantasy, her body is warm and slippery-wet. Her hands are all over him, practically demanding him. But he can't get a picture of her face that isn't severe or sullen, like when he tried to talk to her this morning. The effort to create her face losing itself in pleasure, losing itself in him, is too much. Instead, with a wave of disgust, he sees himself: a peeping Tom, spying through a crack in a bathroom door, lacking word or gesture to justify himself.

NICOL SQUISHES DOWN and wishes the water were blankets and she could go to sleep. When she was fourteen, her friend Lise used to come over before school and wake her up. They would sit on Nicol's bed and have Player's Light cigarettes and orange juice for breakfast. Sometimes they would talk themselves out of going to school and spend the day blending into the shopping mall, people-watching and making plans.

One day Lise woke Nicol by bouncing up and down

on the end of her bed. "Do you want to run away from home?"

Nicol was half-asleep. "Sure."

Then Lise said the magic words: "Don't Think."

Nicol can't remember the names or faces of the people who gave them rides. The first guy asked a lot of questions. It seemed appropriate to lie to him even though he was more interested in asking than hearing the answers.

"Are you gals sisters?"

"Yeah."

"Twins?"

"Well, sort of. We're not really sisters like that."

He asked how old they were, and they answered in unison, a little too quickly, "Sixteen."

"Sixteen means you're legal. You have lots of boyfriends?"

By the time they got to Saskatoon it was getting dark and harder not to think. They had got dropped off near the centre of town, and had no idea how to get back on the main highway. They spent the night huddled together in the foyer of Victory Elementary School. They said a little prayer to the janitor, thanking him for leaving the door unlocked. Lise propped herself up against the radiator, and Nicol curled up against her. They kept their arms around each other and whispered and giggled most of the night. Nicol started singing some song from the radio: "I wanna live like lovers do." Lise answered with her own version, "I wanna die like lovers do." They traded off lines.

"I wanna sigh like mothers do."

"I wanna fry like onions do."

"I wanna live like livers do."

"I wanna lie like your brother does."

And then together, a little too loudly, their version of the last line of the song, "Is it *really* with you?"

Then Lise was whispering again, in a phony accent from no identifiable place, "Hush, hush, sweet Nicolai. We are lovers. I could never leave you." Nicol was giggling in steady waves. They got to sleep eventually.

When she woke up, Lise was slumped against her, still asleep. Lise was breathing noisily, like someone on a hospital soap opera gasping her last breath under an oxygen tent. It was morning in Saskatoon, and Lise was having an asthma attack.

They held hands in the back of the cab. Nicol realized she was breathing slowly and mechanically in rhythm with Lise, as if it were possible to do some of it for her. Lise looked scared because Nicol was. Nicol whispered, "Do not worry, sweet Lisonovitch. It is *really* with us."

At the emergency ward, Lise was taken in a wheelchair down the hall. A nurse asked Nicol a lot of questions and phoned both her parents and Lise's. An old friend of the family whom Nicol could hardly remember came and took her to the bus depot. She bought her breakfast and a nonrefundable ticket home to Winnipeg. Lise's parents were flying into Saskatoon that afternoon.

WHEN NICOL FINALLY gets out of the bath, the music has stopped. She puts the razor blade away in the upper corner of the medicine chest. She gets dressed and yells to Lenny to get ready to go.

Lenny's gone, though. He left a note and the keys to his truck. The note says, "Sorry, Nicky—I had to go meet Ben—an emergency—you know Ben—you'll be fine—Love, Lenny." Nicol reads the note over a few times as if there must be something else in it; a hidden message she's missing.

Nicol gathers up the smaller pieces of the bike and stuffs them in a paper bag. She kicks the other parts into a heap in the corner of the room and piles the frame on top. She is almost out the door when the phone rings. It is Lise calling from Toronto.

"Hey, I'm getting married."

"To Tom?"

"No, to Billy the Kid. Of course to Tom. I want you to be my best man, Nicol."

"Okay, but tell me one thing, Lise. Is it *really* with you?"

They laugh, and Nicol says, "I can't talk. I've got an appointment to make."

"Don't think about it. It'll go away," Lise advises.

"We aren't fourteen any more, Lise. Can't you get that through your head?" Suddenly, Nicol is crying uncontrollably, whimpering and practically bellowing at the same time.

"Shh, shh," Lise is crooning into the phone. "It's okay. Do you want me to come? Is Lenny there? Is it Lenny? I'll come tomorrow if you want. Don't worry. It's good to cry. Do you think you can stop crying and tell me what's wrong?"

Nicol can finally talk. "It's okay, Lise. It's not an emergency. Let's talk about you, okay? Congratulations and all that shit."

They talk about wedding plans for almost half an hour. Nicol has fifteen minutes to make it to the clinic. On the way to the truck, she tosses the bag of bicycle bits into the big blue garbage bin in the parking lot.

LENNY HALF-RUNS, half-walks over to Ben's apartment. He bangs on the door, but there is no one home. He sits down in the hallway and gives the yellow-green, indoor-outdoor carpet a good stare. He doesn't think about the imaginary baby. Instead he sees the bike in his mind, going over bolt by bolt the way he took it apart. He imagines scrubbing down each piece of metal and returning each one to its proper place.

JANE

THEY TOOK JANE TO THE HOSPITAL for trying to get at herself, and Danny wished they'd taken him instead. The first time, Mum and Dad spent almost as much time at the hospital as Jane did. This time, Mum didn't even go with them. Dad took her in the morning before catching his plane to Vancouver.

Jane was pretty bad this time. Her arms and legs were all scabbed and smeared with blood. She picked at the scabs, making them into potholes. Danny asked her what the hell she was doing, and she said, "I'm finding myself." She said it in such a smart-assed way that Danny knew she wasn't anymore crazy than he was. But then she just drew him into another inane conversation.

"You're right here, Jane. Here with me. Your brother Danny."

"Here is where the heart is."

"That's right, you're home."

Then, "Here is where the heart is, here is where the heart is, here is where the heart is," in a flat chant, all the time picking at one great purple scab on her thigh. She stopped chanting when the scab came free, and started fingerpainting on her shorts with the fresh blood. She drew little Xs and Os, which only half came out.

That was yesterday. Now Danny's mother was acting like it was something awful happening to her, not Jane. She was circling the island in the kitchen, just walking, with her hands wrapped around her elbows and her arms folded into her chest. She wasn't a big person. Danny was fifteen and already he was a head taller than her. Usually she seemed big, though. Usually she was rushing around organizing something huge like Sabbath dinner or measuring for new floor-length curtains or just talking, telling everyone what was important and why they should do things her way. You could say she took up a lot of space for her size. But now she was holding onto herself, her shoulders bunched up like she was a homemade doll that was only pinned together and still needed to be sewn up.

Danny felt at once like yelling at her to come back to earth and like touching her back where she was all drawn in, just to prove that she was really solid and strong. Back rubs make everything all right. That's what Jane had told him when he was little and afraid to go to sleep again after a nightmare. She would rub his back, and usually he would sink right back into sleep. Other times, he would be too tense. It would tickle, and he would half-scream, half-laugh, kicking wildly. Then Jane would start tickling in earnest. She really liked tickling him. "Cause and effect. I touch you, you laugh," was how she explained it. He laughed and screamed and always nearly (once did) peed his pants.

She was six years older than Danny and had lots of friends and records. They had parties in the basement; Danny wasn't allowed to go. When Jane was having friends over, Mum and Dad would be especially nice to Danny. Dad would find some treat he'd been saving, like leftover chocolate Hanukkah gelt, and Mum would read to him from his favourite book (which she said she hated), *World's Greatest Hockey Tales*. Now Danny could see that the rotten thing about having a perfect childhood is that it doesn't prepare you for how rotten things are when you're not a kid any more.

Danny couldn't remember when exactly Jane started fading out. Gradually the friends stopped coming over, while Jane settled more and more into the basement. She read books like *The Bell Jar* and listened to the same Joni Mitchell songs over and over. He hated Joni Mitchell's too-high wailing voice pouring into the kitchen from the basement stairs. Bits of her songs would lodge in his head like a stuck record. None of this made him worry about Jane, though. Once when he was nine or ten, he had complained that Jane never played with him any more. Dad said it was just adolescence and she would grow out of it. But Jane seemed to grow into it, not out of it. Mum must have known something was strange. She would constantly suggest activities for Jane. Then Jane would produce a test or essay from school with "Excellent work, Jane" marked on the top and excuse herself downstairs. Even Mum couldn't argue with marks like that.

The first time they took Jane to the hospital was after she stopped going to school and long after they had gotten used to leaving her supper at the top of the basement stairs. She was like a refugee in a strange house where everyone spoke a language she didn't understand. What you don't understand is scary and maybe embarrassing, so gradually she stopped trying, or was it pretending to try, to understand? Danny had felt a mild jealousy at the attention she was getting, but not much more. He got to spend the weekend at Jesse's, and they held the World Table Hockey Championships. They used Jesse's mum's cooking timer to make the games regulation time. Jesse was Sweden, Canada and Florida, and Danny was the U.S., the U.S.S.R. and Check (neither of them could spell Czechoslovakia). Jesse's little brother Dave, whom they called Dumbbell Davie, was the referee.

DANNY REALIZED how little he'd thought about Jane these last few years. She was like a well-loved security blanket; an essential part of childhood that at some unmemorable point gets tossed aside without a backward glance. If you asked him to describe her now, what she was like, what she did, what she liked, he couldn't do it.

When he was little, she'd loved him. She'd try to explain things to him in a way that made everything okay. He had been a crybaby about everything. A leftover birthday balloon would pop, and he'd be in tears.

"Danny, don't be sad. It's great what happened."

"What?"

"That was a special balloon, Danny. All the air inside it was real sad, but strong too. It liked being a big red birthday party balloon for a while, but then it got to be like a trap. All the air inside was in one place while all around the balloon, everywhere really, was all kinds of other air. The balloon could fly about when you batted it, but it could never touch any of the air that wasn't inside with it. It seemed like wherever it went, it never got any closer to the air on the outside. This made it so sad that it decided to get out, no matter how."

"How did it make itself pop?"

"It just held its breath until it puffed up so big it couldn't help but pop."

Danny looked around. "So where is it now?"

"It's all around you, Danny. It's touching with the air on the outside so well that you can't even tell it apart."

Danny spread his fingers and waved his arms slowly up and down. "Is some of it touching me?"

"You and me and Mum and Dad and maybe everybody in Winnipeg soon."

Danny looked at the red rubber fragments in his hand and then to Jane for explanation.

"That part is happy too because its inside can touch its outside and it doesn't have to be all stretched out any more. Look at how red and happy it is, compared to when it was all thin and tense."

He must have been crazy then, because he believed her. For the tenth time he wished it was him who was freaking out now, not Jane. He couldn't have, though. If Jane was her old self and he was going nuts, she would have known just what to say to make everything all right.

DANNY WATCHED his mum go around one more time. Usually he kidded her about wearing too much makeup. She was forty-nine, but you wouldn't know it when she "put on her face." Just a few years ago, a waitress had mistaken Jane and her mum for sisters. She wasn't made-up now, and Danny wished she were. Her face didn't look old, just vague—out of focus. He couldn't look at it for long.

When the phone rang, Danny practically jumped on it.

"Hi, Pritchard. How's it going?"

"Okay, Jesse. What's up?"

"There's a river party tonight and my brother says he'll sell us a quarter-ounce, but you've got to put in ten bucks. Are you coming?"

"Yeah. No. Look, you're going, so if I'm there, you'll know I'm coming," Danny said, instantly out of patience.

"Okay, okay. Keep your shorts on, Danny-Boy. Gee. Do what you want. So long."

Jesse had only recently started talking that way, calling him Danny-Boy or Pritchard and acting like Winnipeg's number-one dope dealer. Last year, he and Jesse were known as the brain brothers or the super geeks in school, but this year Jesse was cool. He cut classes and dressed and walked and talked cool. Danny thought it was dumb, but he caught himself walking that way too—kicking his feet out and taking long slow strides like a cartoon villain— when he was with Jesse.

Mum finally stopped pacing and slid onto the bench in

the kitchen nook. She braced her elbows on the table and held her face up with her hands.

"I'm going out, Mum. You'll be all right?"

"What? Of course, honey," as though she hadn't even heard. Danny thought he would go and get stoned out of his face. On Monday he would go to school and brag like Jesse, "I had such a good time Friday night I don't even remember it."

OUTSIDE, DANNY couldn't believe how easy it was to breathe. Ever since he was little, he'd had asthma. The attacks would come on gradually, so he wouldn't even notice them. His eyes would get wide and he would start to move in slow motion like a person walking under water. Mum or Jane would notice and give him medicine from the "puffer" spray. If it worked, he would be instantly exhilarated. When breathing was so easy, it was almost as if he could get high on air. It was like that song, "you never know what you've got till it's gone." Danny was one step behind that. He never knew what he'd lost until he got it back again.

He also didn't seem to know where he was going until he got there. It was about three miles from River Heights where he lived to the hospital where Jane was, and this was the first time Danny had walked the whole way. The hospital had a separate building for people like Jane. The Elizabeth Dafoe Building tried to look like the rest of the hospital: the same red brick, the same freshly cut and watered lawn, the same pink begonias beside the sidewalk. It managed all right, Danny thought, unless you looked closely. The outside was supposed to be cheery and healthy-looking, but the inside—the silent screamers, the deluded visionaries, the rockers who did nothing but rock back and forth all day every day, and Jane—all seeped through somehow.

JANE IS STILL, sitting in the tweed armchair staring at her green thighs. Her pyjamas look like what Hawkeye wears for surgery on *M*A*S*H*. They are supposed to be loose and comfortable, but the bandages on Jane's thighs are making the pants so tight the seams threaten to split. Her hair is pulled back in a ponytail, and her face is too big. Jane is one of those people who have big lips that jut out too far and look permanently bruised. They make her look like she's trying to look sensitive and serious all the time. Her eyes are wide and her pupils dilated from the medication. She senses her face spread out and around these features, like a lake around islands, in a great wide oval. It's as if her cheeks are just as open as her eyes.

Danny looks at her and then looks away. The trouble is, it is all just space. Eyes, lips, nose, cheeks, chin dimple, none of it forming anything Danny can recognize. None of it is the real Jane.

"Jane?"

She looks up at him just for a second. She seems to have recognized the name, but not him.

"Hey, Jane?"

She is thinking about her face, about the bones that are trying to push through, that just have to get through, only to break up all that smooth face. If the bones can't do it, she thinks she will have to become very old. The smooth stretches of skin will shrivel up and cling to the bone underneath. The face will become one ugly tight mess of dry features, but at least it will be a manageable size. She runs her tongue gently around the inside of her cheek, knowing that if she presses, even a little bit, it will go right through and the cheek will dissolve into pure space.

Danny looks at the person where Jane was and thinks, Whatever happened to Baby Jane? That film is something he'd watched when he was little, and he still has nightmares about it. The final image of Jane's sister lying helpless on the beach, surrounded by happy, oblivious sunbathers, is as vivid now as it ever was. Thinking about a horror movie here, with Jane so sick, embarrasses him, so he can't help smiling. The smile turns into the start of an idea. A crazy idea, but what better place for it? He feels dizzy, like he's just discovered something great. Like he's just discovered he could fly and all he needs is a good take-off point.

"Just hang in there, Jane baby. I'll be right back."

He needs something to get things going. That much is clear. Magic or fuel. Maybe magic fuel. He takes the elevator up to the top floor and then changes his mind and takes it back down to the cafeteria floor. The cafeteria is still open, but it doesn't look very promising. There are a few dried-out-looking sandwiches, no donuts, and some canned drinks sitting in a puddle of water that must have started out as ice. The woman at the cash register is reading a book, a Harlequin, and doesn't even look up when Danny comes in. Danny is about to leave when he spots it. There is a yellow plastic bag on the radiator, ripped open at one end, with the word "GENERIC" written in block letters across it. It is probably empty, Danny thinks, but he picks it up anyway and stuffs it into his pocket. It's a start. He feels like a thief, walking quickly, but not letting himself run to the washroom to examine the thing. No one seems to notice, though. He remembers that you could be dying and helpless on a beach full of people and no one would even notice you. The "GENERIC" bag isn't empty, after all. It has one of those surgical gloves stuck onto one side so you can put it on and peel the yellow plastic off without contaminating the glove.

Jane is still in the chair looking like nothing has changed.

"Jane, talk to me."

Her pupils swim up and actually look at him for a second before they sink back down again.

"Jane, I know how to get you out. Are you coming?"

This time she doesn't raise her head at all, but the room is tense with the effort it takes her not to do so.

"Jane, if you want to get out, you have to let me in."

"You're crazy, Danny." Her voice is slow and hazy, with no intonation, like someone talking in her sleep.

Danny wishes he could explain what they are going to do, but he is still working out the details. A few minutes ago, he felt like a magician. Now he feels childish—the shame of having duped himself into false hope. His humiliation is acutely physical. Sureness of his impending failure to reach Jane courses through his whole body, and his lip begins to twitch rhythmically the way it always did when he was a little kid on the verge of throwing a tantrum.

"Think of something, you idiot kid. Think," Danny says to himself out loud. Maybe a massage, but he is afraid to touch her, afraid she would pull away and then the chance to pull her back would be lost. If the glove is really magic, maybe if he wore it ... she's right. He is crazy. What the hell good could that do? The beigeness of the walls, the tweed stuffiness of the chair and Jane—the room itself seems to be conspiring against him. Even if he and Jane could fly, they'd be able to take off from anywhere except here.

DANNY IS SITTING on the floor now, shredding the yellow plastic off the glove. They are both cross-legged, almost in the same pose. He thought something magic would happen, thought he'd come up with a master plan to get to her. Visiting hours are almost over. Danny is sure they won't ask him to leave. They'll think he is just another patient here.

Jane is still in her trance. She scratches half-heartedly at her thighs, but the bandages don't loosen. Danny finds the opening of the glove in his mouth and starts blowing. He remembers Jane's story about the balloon. Instead of remembering with that warm-sick tenderness, this time he wants to throttle her. She really pulled one over on him that time. He will blow the glove up like a balloon, until it bursts into a million pieces, until there is nothing left. He will blow it up so big that it will break this room apart before it explodes itself.

The glove is hand-size now, but no amount of blowing will make it any bigger. Danny's shortness of breath is increasing with his anger, until finally she snatches the thing away from him.

"For chrissake, Danny, are you trying to give yourself another asthma attack?"

Danny hasn't had an asthma attack since he was twelve, but he keeps quiet about it. The magic seems to be working.

"I want a balloon, Jane."

"Okay. I'll do it," she says, and she does.

The wide spaces on her cheeks get red and round and solid as the glove starts to expand. Her lips take to balloon blowing as if it is their natural vocation. Danny looks up at her and again feels the admiration that only a younger child can feel for an older sibling. When she's finished, she pinches the end and holds it up for him to see. It is perfectly clear and looks like a strange sea creature with four rounded spikes on top and a tail or a pod to one side.

When the attendant leans his head in the doorway and says, "Visiting hours are just about up," Jane is so startled she lets go of the glove. It takes off on a short, frenzied, obscene-sounding flight around the room. Danny can't help giggling, and once he starts he can't stop.

"What's so funny, baby?"

"Cause and effect," Danny sputters. "I giggle, I giggle some more," he says and she starts to laugh as well.

"I giggle, you giggle, he/she giggles."

"It's a giggly little world in here."

At the same time, they remember where they are. Jane pulls her knees up to her chest and lets the film slip down over her eyes.

"Okay, Jane. I'll be back tomorrow if you want," but

she is back in her cocoon, picking at a bandage, and won't answer. "I really will be back."

He is almost sure she gives a little nod. Danny jogs down the corridor and takes the stairs two steps at a time. He puts a quarter in the pay phone and dials automatically.

"Mum?"

"Danny, where are you, honey?"

"Everything's okay, Mum." He's flustered, realizing she won't know what he's talking about. "No. I mean, are you all right? Did Dad call? I mean—"

"Are you at the hospital, Danny? You wait right there. I'll come and get you."

"It's all right, Mum. Really."

"Danny, I'll be there in ten minutes."

Only after he has hung up does he realize how normal she sounded on the phone. She sounded like a mother who could be counted on to take care of everything. Both of them, she and Jane, pop back to life again the minute they forget he's not a kid any more.

Danny goes outside to wait for his mum. It's dark, but the air is warm and sticky. The sky is huge and empty, like a planetarium before the light show starts. Danny leans against the Elizabeth Dafoe Building and looks up straight into space. For once he doesn't feel tall for his age.

Donut Shop Lovers

The Girl at the Donut Shop

Allison is the most beautiful girl at the donut shop. Every morning before 8:30. Coffee with cream. A banana muffin. Heated. Never donuts. No book, no newspaper. She draws stars on her napkin. Five-sided, six-sided, eight-sided. Writes one word: stargazer. Blots it out with drops of coffee from a spoon. Stares out the window, at the counter, at nothing.

Adam is innocuous. A regular guy. Steady. Two iced donuts. Black coffee. Anne Tyler just out in paperback. Pretending not to stare at the bare portion of Allison's legs. The curve of her calf is so radiant it could blot out the sun. Adam is wolfing donuts. Waiting it out.

Adam is thirty-five and a successful architect. He is too urban to pray, but sometimes he silently confides in God. "I'm going to spend the rest of my life loving this perfect girl creature," he tells God. I'm going to make her my shrine. I'm going to give her everything; annihilate myself in her. Sometimes he cajoles God: "If I could just have her for one night, just one afternoon. If I could just touch her face, her hand; if I could sit next to her in the dark of a movie theatre, I wouldn't have to touch her at all." He is lying, begging for whatever he can get. God doesn't say anything.

It happens every day. 8:30 till quarter to 9:00. The girl in the donut shop is growing her hair. Adam notices. He sees her every day. Adam is on the last page. It's only 8:35. Allison is already doodling on her napkin. Maybe she stares at Adam when he isn't looking. Today's the day.

"You can read it if you want. I'm finished."

"No, thanks. I don't."

"Don't what?"

"Don't read."

"Oh." 8:37. Adam has to think of something else to say. He looks at her outright. She is still staring. A blank, marble stare.

"You're here every day."

"Uh-huh. To wake up. You know—coffee. You're always here too. Did you like it?"

"What?"

"You know. The book."

The conversation goes right through them. Words don't matter. Allison knows they will become lovers. Her face is oval, eyes dark brown, wondering, round (Adam's observations). He sits so straight, like it's perfectly natural; like horniness is a moral imperative (Allison's).

Sensation

Adam's apartment is nice. She doesn't go to the donut shop any more. She hasn't been back to her room on Alfred Street, hasn't paid the rent. They must be looking for her. Adam doesn't ask. He is everywhere here. In the bookshelves, on the posters, in the toothpaste on the mirror. Even when he's not home, he's holding her, pushing back the edge. Saving her. She puts her hand under her T-shirt and flattens it against her breast. Her nipples are sore and swollen. She squeezes one and then the other. Sensation. Where is Adam? Allison twists her nipple hard. It feels like a steel pin from her breast to her navel. It holds her there. She wants to stay.

Safeway

Adam's friends are coming over. Jerry and Ellie. Louise and Orb. Everything is arranged. They are dying to meet Allison. Adam is at the supermarket buying wine and garlic butter for garlic bread. Allison is at home making chicken. Everything is fine. He has no reason to be nervous. Last night she washed her hair and braided it into sixteen braids. They'll like her. The dinner will be good. Anyone can make chicken. He can't believe they are living together. Adam and the most beautiful girl in the donut shop. She's so sensitive. Never goes out, hardly ever talks. All he has to do is love her more. Sometimes he thinks there's something wrong with her, with them.

Walking through Safeway: the aisles are wide. It's amazing how many different kinds of crackers there are. How many kinds of everything there is. Adam breathes. He knows where the garlic butter is, but he pushes the cart up and down the aisles anyway. He doesn't want this forward motion to end.

Chicken

All Allison has to do is the chicken. The whole apartment smells like gas. She lights the pilot light on the stove. It flickers and goes out. This has been going on for a while. The raw chicken has goosebumps. Allison hates chickens. They are so stupid and so mean. This chicken is being a real bastard. She could fry it, but she doesn't know the Colonel's secret recipe. This is Canada. She doesn't know any fried chicken recipe. She can't stand the thought of sawing the legs and wings off. Allison puts the chicken back in the oven, pretending the element is on. She opens all the windows.

Like Normal

The dinner is a disaster. They order Champ's Chicken. They laugh about it, but then Allison says it's all her fault. She's such a dunce. She's sorry. "Don't start being a pain in the ass, Allie." Adam, whispering through his smiling teeth. Then she's sobbing. Adam has to hold her, shush her, right there in front of his friends. Pathetic. He wishes he could get into an argument with Orb. Flirt with Ellie. Like before. Like normal. Jerry and Ellie look at Allison and then at each other. They think he doesn't know they know. Orb tries clowning, slobbering over his chicken, making animal noises. "Oooh. It's sooo good." Louise tells him to shut up. Then Louise and Orb do the dishes as if nothing's wrong. Ellie and Jerry keep up the furtive looks. Allison is placed on the window ledge, eyes dried, one leg stretched straight out, toes pointed, looking sad. Fragile. Adam wants them all to go away. Forget the dishes. Leave the talk about Louise's custody fight, about work, about the movies. Just leave and lock the door. He wants to kiss her back to life right there on the window ledge. Suck all her sorrow till it dissolves in his mouth. He can devour it. He has the power.

 Finally enough time has passed, and Adam's friends can leave. "A lovely girl, Adam." Orb winks. Condescending bastard. "Thanks so much." "Give us a call." He can barely endure it. The door clicks shut.

The You Think I Think Conversation

In time, they fall into patterns like other couples.

Allison on the passenger side, stocking feet, knees pulled up against her, twisting a strand of hair around and around. Resisting putting it in her mouth. Childish.

Adam driving. Feeling only rage. They both have their eyes on the road. "You always think I'm not on your side. Like I'm the enemy or something. I go to work, and you think I'm abandoning you. You think I like being there? Do you think I lie awake at night thinking of ways to make you feel bad?"

"No. No. Did I say that? I'm just ... you get so far away, I think you hate me. I do. I think you hate me sometimes because you think ..."

"I don't hate you. I don't think anything like that, Allison. Do you always have to make something out of nothing? Can't you just let it go?"

"No," Allison says to herself. "No means no." Someone told her that once. The woman who looked after her when her mother wasn't there. Vanished without notice. Her mother always returned "refreshed." A little bit lighter. Hollows in her cheeks hollower. "You see, I always come back, I'll always come back," she would say, convincing herself, but not Allison. Allison had to reassure her: "Of course you came back. You're such a silly mother and you do look refreshed. Prettier, even." Her mother would call her the perfect child, tuck her in and read to her. Allison would curl up in bed, suck her hair and listen to her mother's excited voice: "And then, do you know what happened?" Until the next time.

No means no. Allison is never going to let it go.

"Allison, wake up. At least pretend to pay attention." Adam has been talking. His side of the story. "What's the point," he says. "What's the point." He sees that there is no way out. He just drives. Her body is lodged in the passenger seat. He turns the wheel, slows, changes gears. "You could at least sit normally," he says. "Come on. Sit up."

Allison moans. A low, trembling moan. She's trying to look like she's trying not to cry (Adam's theory).

"Come on, Allie. Please don't cry. I didn't mean anything bad. Come on. Enough."

Adam brakes hard for a rabbit that crosses a few feet ahead of them without even looking. Just missed it. Allison sits straight up and they both stare at the highway, looking for the rabbit, but it's long gone.

"God. That would have been a real mess."

"Yeah."

They forget about themselves long enough to feel better, lighter. Allison is hungry.

"It's nice to get out of the city sometimes." Allison, sounding normal.

"But it's a long drive." Adam slows down for the turnoff. Everything seems to be all right.

Donut Shop Lovers

"Let's tell each other the truth about ourselves, always." Allison staring straight at his wide-open eyes.

"Alright." Adam watching the perfect open-almost-closed motion of her lips.

"If your feelings for me change or whatever. Let's never be afraid to say it."

"Alright." Adam smothering conversation in a movie kiss. Circa 1946—a long one. No fade-out. Sex isn't dirty. Adam and Allison close the door on time. Pull the shades on everyone else. Lock the cat in the kitchen. Passion isn't phony. It lasts forever while it's lasting. The sheets are falling off the bed. The air is thick like Thunder Bay on a foggy night.

"If we die here, let's be reincarnated as mushrooms. The atmosphere is perfect." Adam looking up from licking Allison's toes, looking for a graceful way to bring his mouth closer, getting lost in the back crevice of a knee.

"You're crazy." Allison's hands on his penis. Direct action. It's easy, pulling him inside her still not completely hard, and the only sound is the slushy sound of impact. They can see their breath. It's tacky to talk about quantity. At some point they fall asleep. Wrapped like a Christmas present in each other's arms.

You Have to Wait
Till Valentine's Day

Indelible ink

YOU PROBABLY DON'T KNOW any Von Shackleburgs. It seems impossible that anyone named Von Shackleburg ever existed. Especially in Germany in 1939. If they did exist, it is even more unbelievable that they would have survived the Holocaust and gone on to produce offspring. My father did, though his name was originally just "Shackleburg." He took on the "Von" as a symbol of the gratitude he felt for the family, the Von ---s, who saved his life by pretending he was their son. My father hates Germans, especially (he once told me) the Von ---s, whose kindness was equalled only by their stupidity and surpassed only by their fanaticism as Christians. They baptized my father, saying a submission to Christ was the sole thing that could save him. Not his life, but him. He didn't submit easily. They had to do it at home in the bathtub because a church baptism of a seven-year-old boy would have aroused suspicion, in both the congregation and the priest, who, like them, was a vocal Nazi supporter. My father threw a tantrum as he stood up to his knees in the holy tap water. They thought he was carrying on because the water was too cold. Mrs. Von --- dumped a bucket of scalding water into the tub, giving him third-degree burns. The resulting purple marks, which still spread across his legs like spilled ink, are something he doesn't mention. Most of his friends have carefully printed numbers on their arms. Souvenirs of Auschwitz or some other chamber of horrors. My father's arms are free of memorabilia.

Mickey Mouse Sorry. I'm getting off-topic. I only mentioned Dad so you would understand about my name. That isn't the most important thing. I don't have a father complex. Actually, I'm quite normal. I'm twenty-one and I'm in Education, which isn't such a Mickey Mouse faculty as everyone says.

The most important thing Something important did happen to me, though. I really don't know how to put it nicely.

You could say I lost something, but it's nothing. Or maybe I got something like love, but one or two gradations below.

That isn't much, either. Things that are almost love are like forgeries. Have I stimulated your curiosity? In my Child Development class, they say that's the most important thing. Don't worry. I won't keep you in the dark much longer. I'm getting to it. (*It.* That's a clue.)

The perfect couple

Another thing that isn't that important but that you might want to know about is what I look like. Nobody believes I'm Jewish, because I have freckles and long straight blonde hair that drives me crazy whenever I try to do anything athletic. I'm not fat or anything and I'm kind of tall. A beautiful girl, right? That's what my boyfriend, Jamie, thinks. We've been going around together for three years. He's a really nice guy, and please don't get nauseated when I tell you that everyone thinks we are the perfect couple. Whenever we go out to a party or a social, our friends are always eyeing my left hand for an engagement ring. I'm not going to go on and on about Jamie and how *his* blond hair covers one eye all the time, even when he's driving, or how disappointed my dad is that Jamie isn't Jewish. I've said enough about Jamie.

Guilt

Jamie can't understand why my father is so disappointed that Jamie isn't Jewish. He doesn't understand my father at all. I probably don't either. My father is always telling me how things are. His method is guilt; his medium, history. I don't see how anyone could argue with that. All my life he has told me I'm lucky because I'll never know what it's like to live in constant terror; to be a Jew blessed with Christian fools to keep you alive. If we see one of those amazing pink sunrises that happen on the prairies, he tells me it's nothing. A sunrise can't truly be appreciated unless you went to bed the night before, praying to be allowed to die in your sleep rather than face the hell of another day. But when you see the sun, somehow you find strength again. When you see the sun, he says, you see God.

God

Anyway, I grew up in River Heights and I never saw God. I never expected to. It's not that I don't believe, because I do. It's just that I have enough sense to realize that God isn't lurking behind every quaint antique lamppost on my street. God, like Education, is not a Mickey Mouse affair. God likes to come out for a good show, but nothing very awe-inspiring has happened in my life, and I doubt it ever will.

So I never saw God, and getting back to the point, I never planned to do "it" either. It isn't that I'm stuck up; I know girls who have been doing it since grade seven, girls and their boyfriends who were doing it between classes in the caretaker's room in junior high. I don't think they're trashy or anything. It's just that it doesn't seem worth risking bringing children into the world. They would either grow up like me, not even capable of appreciating a sunrise, or in some hell like my father's or worse. I'm one of those girls who believed what they said in Health class about abstinence as the only reliable form of birth control. Besides, I'm sure I would die in labour. My hips aren't that wide, and I'm a total wuss when it comes to pain.

It

It must be time to spell it out. This is a story about how all that rational, sensible resolve in the last paragraph disappears into thin air. If this story were an essay, I'd flunk for not getting to the topic sentence until halfway through. I bet you are wondering whether Jamie, the perfect boyfriend, is responsible for what happens. I'm wondering too.

The big event

Jamie drives me around a lot, which makes me feel guilty since there are times when I find his car more interesting than him. On the morning of the big event, I was waiting on the steps for Jamie to pick me up and give me a ride to school. He is punctual, which is a valuable quality a lot of people overlook. I got in the car and we kissed. His kisses are like pleading; mine are vacant lots. His mouth is all soft and giving in, wet like a puppy's and always wanting more. I don't know what to do with my mouth. I try to balance it against his and not let both of us start to melt. This particular morning he was extra passionate, kind of clawing at me. I thought, another thing I like about his car is that it's a standard. The stick shift makes that kind of groping really awkward. He has a sense of propriety, he's considerate really, so we got going after not too long.

Fornicating

I'm really running on at the mouth now. Jamie's car has *nothing* to do with what I want to tell you. When we got to school, Jamie was looking for a parking space, and I was looking for an excuse to have an hour to myself before class. Did I mention Jamie's in all my classes? This was when Jamie told me he thought we should "talk." This surprised me. My dad always wants to "talk" to me. Usually he starts out with a description of something that happened in the concentration camps that is so horrible I can't even imagine it. The last one was about people, brothers and sisters sometimes, fornicating openly in cramped cells full of filthy, starving men, women and children. The point again was how lucky I am that I can live a decent life, that I should be thankful I don't know *true* suffering, and be grateful I've never been reduced to an animal who has to claw away at anyone, even his sister, for a moment of feeling alive. (Translation: that boyfriend of yours isn't even Jewish. I hope to God you don't bring *that* kind of shame on your family.) That's my father, but Jamie and I aren't big talkers. I didn't know what he wanted to talk about, but I could tell it wasn't going to be fun.

Talk

Jamie and I stayed in the car. We turned to face each other and he put his hand over mine. Jamie has brown eyes that always look sincere and a peaches-and-cream complexion. One of his eye teeth is crooked, overlapping the next tooth. This tooth is his only obvious flaw, and when he started talking, I had trouble concentrating on what he was saying. I wanted to reach out and push the tooth into line with the others.

"Shelley," he started off, his eyes zipping back and forth between our hands and my face, so I couldn't help but notice again how sincere his eyes look. I was expecting the worst. Something horribly sentimental like, "You know I can't make it without you, ____." (Fill in the blank with the appropriate endearment: a) baby; b) honey; c) sugar pie.) Then it would have taken all my power to maintain a calm, reassuring expression on my face.

Yogurt

Instead, I got, "I know you don't love me, Shelley. You should, but you don't. I think we should break up." His voice was shaking like a scared little boy's who is announcing to his mother that he's running away from home. If I had reached over and hugged him, he would have melted all over me. He would have told me he didn't mean it. We could have held hands and walked into the Education lounge. Before class we could have talked about whether we should wait until after we graduate to get engaged, about our chances at getting jobs in the city or near each other in the country. Our future is such a safe subject that I can believe in it, the same way I believe that the next time I open the fridge there will be at least two flavours of yogurt to choose from. The way I believe that what happened to my father, to his family, cannot happen any more, never did happen, because I cannot imagine it.

I thought about all the times I'd sworn up and down to Jamie that I really do love him, the times I argued just because I won't "have sex" doesn't mean we aren't lovers. I was having trouble focussing. The most I could say was, "Jamie, don't tell me how I feel. Don't tell me I don't love you."

"Shelley, it's not your fault. You're screwed up. I love you, but I'm tired of this."

"This. What *this*? Are you tired of me? You don't love me any more so you tell me I don't love you. Take some responsibility, Jamie." This was meant to be my trump phrase. How could he accuse me of not loving him when given the impossible task of proving he *really* loves me?

"I love you, Shelley, but I'm leaving you." He said it word by word, like he was engraving the sentence in his mind.

I had nothing to say. I saw the world gaping around me, devoid of Jamie. I was relieved. I was petrified. I didn't believe him. "What do you want from me?"

His whole body was tense and his face was deep red. My fingers were white and my hand hurt where he gripped it. Jamie was angry.

"I want you to be human. Maybe it's not your fault, Shelley, but you're faking it. You're a pretty girl, but that's all."

There was a moment of stunned silence during which both of us marvelled at how Jamie could know and say so much. Eventually, I thought of saying, "Same to you, Lambkin," and slamming the door, strolling nonchalantly away, but the dramatic moment was already lost by the time I thought of it.

Truth

I said instead, "Fine, Jamie, fine. You're entitled to your opinion," and got out of the car.

Jamie pulled the lever on the bucket seat and lay back in the car, his anger, the only anger I'd ever seen in him, spent. He said, "Wait, Shelley . . . " I slammed the door.

Enough about Jamie. I mean it this time. I had to get away from him as fast as I could. I left him with his one sentence of truth. It was better than hanging around and giving him the chance to take it back.

Walking

Walking. I couldn't stop. Down Pembina Highway with the wind blowing my hair across my face. For the last three years Jamie and I probably drove down Pembina Highway at least three times a week. It's the fastest way to get to school and the ugliest street in the whole city. I wondered how I should feel, walking the strip for the first time without Jamie. McDonald's, Burger King and Wendy's, all crouched together at the same intersection, their plastic weatherproof skin glaring RED, ORANGE, YELLOW, respectively. Then the Pony Corral, which despite its name had great rootbeer floats and real hamburgers. (Now it's a discotheque where the waitresses wear a cross between exercise leotards and Playboy Bunny suits.) Next was the Pink Flamingo Motel, which really is pink and really has a greater-than-life-size plastic flamingo perched over the semi-burned-out neon sign. Then the car dealers, Pontiac, Chev Olds, Nissan, all the same tin boxes. Deathtraps, all of them, according to my father.

Waiting

The ugliness was overwhelming. I kept walking. My father says there is nothing worse than waiting. He should know, but I bet the people who had to walk from one camp to the next or until they dropped thought walking was worse. It's so slow it's almost a kind of waiting.

After a long time I got somewhere: the cement park at Confusion Corner, which is at the end of Pembina Highway and the beginning of downtown. The park is modern. There are no trees, no grass, no swings, not even a fountain. There is a cement sculpture-thing, big cement wedges for leaning on, and that's all. You can think of

Spiderman

it as an experiment that failed. It is so not school, not home and not Jamie. Not human, like me, I thought; then I saw someone watching me. He was young, and his curly hair was too long. He looked like a juvenile delinquent—old blue jeans, a yellow T-shirt with the YMCA emblem so faded it was barely recognizable and great big running shoes with the laces undone in the current teen fashion. He was crouched like a spider on the edge of one of the cement embankments, just staring.

According to my all-knowing father, not everything that happens has a reason. Hopefully I'm getting close to the reason for telling you all this.

"Hi," I said. (Can you believe I had the nerve to talk to him?)

He jumped up and loped over to sit by me, showing off his long spider legs. "I was watching you because I thought you were a friend of mine. You look like her—you know, the blonde hair—but you ain't her. Sure is a fuckin' ugly park. Want a cigarette?" he said, the words tripping over each other like his feet probably did with those laces.

"I don't smoke, thanks," I said.

"Good thing, 'cause I don't got any cigarettes," he said and belted out a laugh. There was a hysterical quality to his voice, and he was so skinny that he was almost all edges. Up close I could see that he was at least my age or older, and that he wasn't about to act it.

"Yer nice," he said.

"You're nice too," I said, for lack of anything better to say, and took one quick desperate look around to see if there was anyone or anything to stop us. There was

75

nothing around except the grey cement walls of the park.

"Come on. I've got my own place, just over behind the school. Come on. I'll show you. I've got some smokes there." On the way he talked incessantly about himself, his description punctuated with abrupt, loud laughs. He was tossing words out like he had an endless supply. He was too jittery to be shy or to really look at me or to realize how weird it is to invite someone you don't even know to your apartment.

I wondered if he would evaporate after we'd done it, or if he would stay to haunt me.

"Here it is, what a great dump, eh?" He was grinning, out of breath from talking so much, and just barely managed to suppress another explosion of laughter. He touched my back to point me in the right direction and ducked as he led us into the basement suite.

The place was tiny and packed with stuff. The ceiling was so low that he had to keep his head bent forward whenever he was standing up. One enormous tabby cat was sprawled across the kitchen table. It yawned at us, but didn't make a move. Two kittens were attacking a roll of toilet paper. When they saw us they started to cry and ran over and jumped on his foot. He tried to lightly kick them off, but they clung to his shoelaces like it was a matter of life and death.

"Great dump," he said again, to fill in a space where he wasn't talking. "You got yer own place? I love it. I ain't never going back."

His questions were just part of the monologue, and I liked that. There was never time to answer. "Back where?" I asked.

"Yeah, back where," he said, laughing again. "I talk too much. The big cat on the table is Mathilde. She's the mother. The kittens are Jack and Jill. I forgot to introduce everyone. I'm Teddy. Teddy Bear. That's my real name. Can you believe my parents would do that to me? Shit."

Teddy Bear pushed some dishes, newspapers and dirty clothes off the bed and we sat down there because there was no place else to sit. The kittens had come for the ride on Teddy's foot. He pushed them off and took his shoes off. The kittens started to cry again and after a few attempts climbed up on the bed.

Teddy said, "Shhh. Jack and Jill, go climb a hill. Get lost. Big joke. There's no hills in this town. Asshole of the universe is what this place is. Fuckin' cold or fuckin' hot all the time." He locked the kittens in a cupboard, where they started to cry in earnest, scratching frantically at the door. Mathilde turned her head to where the noise was coming from, then fixed her green stare on us.

It at last

What was it like? His ribs were marvellously wide, skin stretched like a drum. You could say he talked me into it, because he talked almost the whole time. As for me, I'm not superstitious, but it seemed as if I was astral projecting while it was happening. I was one of those hidden cameras crouching in the corner of the ceiling, watching the spiderman work. "God, shoulders," Teddy said, clearly amazed that I had them. "Oh wow. Those kittens better shut up. This is amazing. Do you like this? Do you like me? Do you want me to shut the hell up?" But he didn't.

We undressed to his babbling, and then he was inside me, fast, like he'd tripped on his laces and just fallen into place. It hurt a little bit, so I knew it was finally happening to me. There were a few seconds where he couldn't talk. He was in a frenzy, thrashing against me like a crazy person throwing himself against a padded wall. He shuddered, said something, or rather, moaned something, then it was over. I stopped watching, and hugged him as if I was trying to crush him. He was so sharp. I wanted to make the imprint of his body against mine permanent, to have purple bruises where each rib cut across me. While I hugged him, there was no noise. Mathilde was still staring at us and the kittens must have either suffocated in there or gone to sleep. It didn't take Teddy long to start babbling again.

"Oh God, don't never go away. I don't even know your beautiful name. Don't move. I'll be right back. Don't move. I got a surprise for you."

He was circling the room. I closed my eyes and felt my body shaking. It seemed my heartbeat was coming from lower than it ever had before. I was afraid to look in case there was blood.

Shit

"Shit," he said, knocking something over. "Keep your eyes closed. I'm looking for a surprise. Jesus H." His voice was getting more hysterical.

When I opened my eyes I saw him crouched between the fridge and the counter as if he was trying to hide something—himself. He pulled one hand behind his back, almost losing his balance, and our eyes met. We saw each other completely naked—raw and vulnerable like circus animals who have been shaved of their fur, stripped of their wildness and put on display for the amusement of humans.

Teddy was cornered. He wiped his mouth and his nose with the back of his hand and cleared his throat. He kept staring at me, bewildered, until a huge grin covered up whatever he was feeling. I couldn't stand to look at him.

"Teddy, get up. What are you doing there?"

"I told you not to look. Now you don't get no surprise. You have to wait till Valentine's Day. Hey, don't go. Come on. Did I hurt you? Shit."

Love

Outside it was cold and getting late. I put the quarter in the phone and dialled automatically.

"Hi."

"God, I looked all over for you. I wanted to say—"

"You have to believe me. I love you, Jamie. I do."

"Say it again."

"I love you, Jamie."

"I'm starting to believe you. I never wanted to break up. I didn't mean—"

"Jamie, can you come and pick me up?"

"Well, yeah. As soon as I finish helping Mum. She just wants me to move a few things down to the basement."

"Fine. Great."

I bet you guessed that Jamie and I are engaged now. My dad didn't freak out too much when we told him. He made a kind of joke about it. He said, "I'm allowing one goy in the family, that's all," but he's started inviting Jamie over for Friday-night dinners. I'm not any different than I was before. Anyway, I'm going on the pill. After a month it's supposed to be safe. Sometimes in a movie theatre or some place like that, I hear someone laughing helplessly; out of control. Usually I'm with Jamie and we just stare harder at the screen, as if that horrible sound has nothing to do with us.

LATERAL MOVES

My son is four and he can spell lamb and baseball. He hates girls but still likes to play with them. When he grows up, he wants to be good. He thinks a lot about Spiderman, chocolate chips and knowing everything. He believes that God is everywhere, but doesn't feel implicated or oppressed or terrified by that faith. I tell him that he is Jewish, Christian, Canadian and American, and he is happy to be so much.

This year he has decided that when he grows up he will marry his friend Zoe, then he will marry a boy, and then he will live alone. When I ask him more about growing up, he changes the subject: "You're old and you're going to die soon, right, Mom?" I tell him most mothers don't die until their children have been grown-ups for a long time. I tell him I plan to be a grandmother before I die.

My son has never been rushed to emergency for stitches or a broken arm. He has never fallen out of a tree or been bitten by a dog. Nobody he loves has ever disappeared or gone mad or died. He once fell in the deep end and spent seven or eight slow-motion seconds upright, almost rigid, with his head just under the surface, his shorts a yellow water balloon, his arms splayed just under the surface of the water and his legs marching foolishly and helplessly up and down. He looked like a little zombie boy on a late-night B movie. Zombies are stuck with lateral moves—they don't know how to raise their arms and faces and their nasty, decaying little souls towards Heaven; they don't know how to die.

Anyway, my son knew I would save him. There was never any question.

"Mom, you won't be a grandmother for a long time, right?"
 "Right."
 He takes my head in his hands and puts his mirror face right up to mine. "Let's not think about that now," he says.

STAINED LEATHER & OTHER ACTS OF GOD

LIKE BLOWN GLASS

EVERY DAY IN JUNE, Karl cornered Mom or Dad and asked, "Could you argue in a court of law that three thousand miles each way constitutes child abuse?" But when Mom and Dad had made up their minds to do something, even something as horrifying as going on a family camping trip all the way to the Bay of Fundy, there was no way to reason with them.

Karl was fourteen and hitting adolescence in that slightly ludicrous, self-righteous way that clever, unpopular boys do. "You couldn't pay me to sit in the back seat with those two brats," he said. Mom ignored him. Dad said, "Always keep your sense of humour, son."

Sarah and Lizzy had no questions. Sarah, who was nine, knew Mom and Dad wouldn't let her bring her best friend, Katie. Last year she had threatened to scream all the way to Sudbury and they had still said there wasn't enough room for Katie. Lizzy, who was considered the baby even though she was only a year younger than Sarah, didn't ask questions. She was a whiner but not a troublemaker, and she liked the idea of Sarah having to sit next to her in the car for six weeks.

As soon as school was out, Mom and Dad packed up the Valiant and they all set out. Dad said they could take

Highway One from Winnipeg all the way to New Brunswick. There they would find the Atlantic Ocean. They would swim in the Bay of Fundy, which boasted the strongest tides in the world.

In North Hatley, Quebec, they stopped to stay with a famous poet who was a friend of Dad's. North Hatley was a magical town. While they were there, Dad took a weekend side trip to Montreal and came back a free man.

This family camping trip was designed to cure him of her, but every day away made him more lovesick for Wendy. She was nineteen, understood poetry, and had hair even curlier than Sarah's. He called her from a Provigo parking lot on the outskirts of Montreal.

"Paul?"

"Come to Montreal. I love you. I can't live without you. Come to Montreal."

It wasn't a decision. She was summoned and she went. She picked up the ticket he bought for her at the airport counter. She barely had time to leave a message for her friend, Nora, asking her to feed the cat. She and Paul spent the weekend at the Hotel Paris, a charming little fleabag on Saint Denis. The bed was lumpy, and the bedding grey and smelling of other tourists. The window faced the red brick of another building, but she and Paul didn't do a lot of sightseeing. On Monday morning, Wendy was curled up on the bed with her eyes closed and her head in Paul's lap when he called Sally. He explained the coersive, relentless nature of genuine love when one is lucky enough to stumble across it, and that he and Wendy would be coming to collect the children in a few days.

Mom went into what grown-ups call shock. Karl told her not to go berserk on them. She screamed at him, "Finally it's my turn. Enough martyr shit. He can't stop me. None of you can stop me." She had known about Wendy, one of Paul's pet students (he'd described her as gifted, and she knew well enough what that meant), but right now did not seem like the obvious moment for her marriage to end. She'd thought they'd had an understanding. The idea was to wait until the kids were grown, not to get dumped by the side of the road halfway through her life.

When Mom wasn't screaming, she was on the famous poet's couch crying, smoking and repeating, "Seventeen years. I gave him seventeen years."

"She needs time," the famous poet's wife told Karl, Sarah and Lizzy. "She'll recover. You'll see. She'll be better off. In a few months, everything will be all right again."

The children did not see. They could imagine knights, monsters, moon visits and fairy princesses as well as the next kid, but they were at a loss when it came to major variations on their own futures. At this point, they could not even imagine the present very well.

Karl spent the time in North Hatley organizing his little sisters and the neighbourhood children. They played "Hide and Seek and Destroy" from after breakfast until bedtime. The French kids had to call Karl "Sir," and the English kids, including Sarah and Lizzy, had to call him "Monsieur." They played in their yards, in the park and even in the lake. They were obsessed with hats—baseball caps, cowboy hats, toques—anything they could find to put on their heads. One neighbourhood kid wore his little brother's yellow diaper cover on his head. He looked fierce. They played without time or tomorrow or language barriers or disputes. The game was intricate, but fluid, and resumed each morning when they all met at the playground by the lake after breakfast.

MOM STAYED ON at the poet's house for a few weeks while she took a glass-blowing workshop at the Artists' Co-op in Sherbrooke. She and the poet collaborated on glass poems—loopy Suess-like bottles with no actual openings and a few of the poet's carefully chosen words etched on each piece. The poet and the other glass-blowers were supportive of Mom. It was the early seventies, and spiritual journeys were in. "Find yourself," everybody counselled. "You have to take this as a sign that now is the time to find out who you really are."

THE CAMPING TRIP continued, with Wendy singing camp songs in the Mom-spot in the car. The first night of the new arrangement, instead of the usual rocky campground and smelly, gaping outhouse, they splurged on a motel room with a queen-sized bed, a double bed and a fold-out cot. Lizzy and Sarah lay on the double bed together, attuned to the danger of toenails. Normally Sarah would have marked a centre line in the bed and threatened Lizzy with a slow, painful death if she crossed it. Lizzy would have unconsciously crossed the line because she always wanted to be where Sarah was. Often she wanted to be Sarah. Also, she needed to annoy her big sister, and her younger-sister instincts told her Sarah needed to be annoyed. But tonight Sarah did not establish boundaries. Everyone was on best behaviour, playing dead, even Karl, who still wasn't speaking to Wendy or Dad. On the cot, Karl was rigid, but Lizzy could tell by his breathing that he was not asleep. Dad and Wendy were huddled together in the middle of the queen-sized bed. They formed one compact lump, which, in the darkness, looked to Lizzy like a single bulging eye; the eye of a sea monster perhaps. Lizzy no longer believed in monsters, but, all the same, she wouldn't look at it. The bad thing, the forbidden thing, was to think about their mother. It was more than bad; it was impossible. There was no spot in the room for her.

IN THE MORNING, they had breakfast at a truck stop by the motel. Lizzy and Sarah usually hated eating breakfast. Today, they were allowed to order Sugar Pops, which came in individual serving-size boxes, and chocolate milkshakes. For most of the breakfast, Dad was beaming at Wendy and speaking gently to the children. He rarely spoke to anyone at length, and the children often felt invisible around him. For the moment, his happiness was contagious.

"Good milkshakes?"

"Mmmm," they said, trading the whole other life they had known and the love of their mother for the cold, sweet taste of chocolate shakes.

IN THE CAR Lizzy and Sarah learned all the camp songs Wendy knew. They had always wanted to go to camp. Karl counted American licence plates and tried to stay silent all the way to New Brunswick and back to Winnipeg—nearly five thousand miles. He counted 467 American cars between Quebec City and St. John's, but he broke down and started talking on the way home. Wendy kept asking him questions about what kind of cars he liked, what he thought about Quebec independence, and if he'd ever seen the Bay of Fundy. She had no opinions of her own, but seemed overly interested in his. He found her easy to talk to, especially when their conversations meant preventing Lizzy and Sarah from enlisting her to sing "Do Your Ears Hang Low" with them one more time. Dad drove in a Buddha-like bliss. The children were used to his sudden rages, and did not find his new calmness reassuring. They only knew he wasn't mad *now*.

THEY ARRIVED HOME at seven in the morning. Wendy was the only one who had never been in the house before, but after a marathon fifteen-hour drive from North Bay the previous day, they all staggered in like survivors exploring an unknown island.

It was strange to be home. The couple who had stayed in the house over the summer had altered things in a way that made Lizzy hate them. They left a photograph of an unknown child on the refrigerator under Mom's banana magnet. They left an ashtray in Lizzy and Sarah's room and a grey sock balled up in the crack between the cushions on the couch. Karl discovered the relic of Sarah's once beloved "blankee" crumpled and stiff in the back of his closet. It had been used as a paint rag.

The couple had also left two kittens as a "thank you for letting us crash here" gift. Karl devised a method of naming the kittens: he sat one of the girls on his shoulders clutching a dictionary. He then spun madly around the room until she admitted she was scared. He kept spinning until she threw the dictionary on the floor, being careful to make it land open, and screamed, "Karl is the King. May he live forever. Master, teach me, teach me." Then the other girl chose a word she didn't know from the open page, and that was the kitten's name. The game went well. No one was hurt, and the kittens were named Habitat and Holocaust. The dictionary was not irreparably damaged or even seriously torn. Habitat was white and ratty-looking and sucked the fur on her paws until it was matted and oily. Holocaust mewed steadily and tried to suck on Habitat's nipples.

The next day, Dad and Wendy bought a waterbed, and that evening, they set it up in the dining room. No one ever ate in there, anyway. Everyone watched the mattress fill up with water. The kittens were especially curious. They kept stretching their little paws along the plastic, and Dad kept pushing them away from the bed. Lizzy took Habitat in her lap and whispered to her, "Just stay here with me, kitty, kitty," but she squirmed away and was sniffing at the bed again. "Do they really use cats to make Chinese food?" Karl asked.

"Could be," Dad said. "Could be."

That night one of the kittens' claws managed to make a leak in the waterbed. Dad used the patching kit that came with the bed to fix it, but then he put Habitat and Holocaust in a box and took them somewhere in the car. While he was gone, Karl and Lizzy and Sarah camped around the waterbed while the patch dried. The mattress's plastic skin was naked and clear without its sheets. There were tiny air bubbles between the plastic and the water. Karl devised a game called "Herd the Bubbles," in which Sarah, Lizzy and Karl tried to amass bubbles each in their own corner of the mattress. Karl chose the corner with the most bubbles nearby, so at first he was winning, but then Sarah discovered that by pounding on the bigger bubbles, she could break them up into smaller ones and get more than Karl. Lizzy was particularly fond of one bubble that seemed oval rather than round. She was afraid it would be broken up, or swallowed by a larger bubble. She talked to it in a crooning voice and gently moved it around her corner.

SARAH'S BEST FRIEND, Katie, once told her that if you don't say the Lord's Prayer every night you'll burn in hell, so at night, Sarah and Lizzy secretly whispered what they knew of the Lord's Prayer before going to sleep. Lizzy suggested getting out of bed and kneeling on the floor as she had seen children do in the *Illustrated Children's Bible*, the only children's book at their doctor's office. Sarah considered it, but thought it was too risky. "They could just come in and see us."

"They won't come in here," Lizzy said. "And besides, we could just say we were looking for a contact lens."

"What about Karl? He could come in."

So they were cautious and prayed lying down, looking up at the mildew lines on the ceiling. Lizzy planned to lie awake after and silently say some of her own special "I dare you / if you're there" prayers, but she couldn't think of anything, not even, "I want my Mommy," or "Let Wendy's Mom bring cottage-cheese pie with strawberries for dinner," or "Make Katie and Sarah let me walk home from school with them." She could think of nothing that she wanted, and lying there she could hear the splash and slosh of the waterbed downstairs. It was a steady sound, like water slapping against a boat in a harbour, except that there was also a moaning and sometimes a barely audible giggling sound. Not long ago, the waterbed noises were scary and unknown, but already they had become as familiar as a bedtime story or the hum of the television in Karl's room next door.

MORE THAN FOUR months after Wendy took over the Momspot, Dad was still obsessed with cleaning up and clearing out. He had transformed his rage into housekeeping duties. He wanted to wipe out all traces of "her." Often, the children woke up early in the morning to the sounds of Dad's efforts to purge and renew. This morning, they hung around watching him scraping at the paint splotches on the living room hardwood. Last year, she had painted the baseboards an unobtrusive pale yellow. The spots on the floor were hardly visible, but Dad was pouring solvent on them and going at them with steel wool. The wood looked raw, like it had open sores where the spots used to be. He didn't talk, except once to tell Karl to move out of the light. Sarah, Karl and Lizzy jumped when he spoke. They wondered what part of his rage they had caused. In fact, he was annoyed that they were so poorly brought up that none of them offered to help. They felt their crime was far graver. They must have done something terrible, like reminding him of "her."

When he was finished with the living room, he moved

on to the basement. He hauled up boxes of "her" things to dump into the aluminum garbage pails next to the garage. She had used the basement as her workshop for all kind of crafts, but her most recent obsession had been glass-blowing. The last year they all lived together, she called the basement her "glass studio" and forbade the children to enter. They hadn't cared about what she was doing down there, but had enjoyed thinking of requests that she would deem important enough to pull her away from the glass studio and back to the main floor, where the children dominated; where their toys, stuffed animals and games were littered about, and their shrieks, their needs, their disputes and their continuing debate about fairness had permeated every room.

KARL ANNOUNCED that he was going to school now. Sarah and Lizzy realized that it was 8:30 and they were still in their pyjamas. Upstairs, Sarah put on the blue school tunic that was no longer mandatory, but in style for grade four. Lizzy picked the shiny striped dress with the green collar and cuffs made by her mother for her seventh birthday. She loved the smoothness of the fabric and the gold sailor buttons, each imprinted with a tiny anchor. The dress was clearly too small. The sleeves were now three-quarter length and pulled at the shoulders whenever she moved her arms, but she liked the fact that it was now a "mini-dress," with the hem well above her knees. She got dressed standing in the closet, with Sarah's clothes hanging neatly on the left and hers on the right. She considered not going to school and spending the day in the closet, curled up on a cushion of red velvet pinafores, but Sarah said, "Come on. I'll walk with you." Usually, Sarah walked with Katie, but it was too late for that today.

They went out the back door and past the garbage pails overflowing with leather scraps, patches of cloth, pieces of cardboard and half-used sketching pads. There was so much Mom had started or planned to start, but in the garbage pails it all looked convincing as garbage. Lizzy and Sarah walked to school through the park and the Witchy Paths. Even though it was scary to walk through the tangled scrub that made up the paths, they always walked this way now. A few weeks ago, they had seen a white cat here they were sure was Habitat. She was bigger than Habitat had been, but kittens have a way of growing into cats. They stopped and stared at the cat, and she stared back at them, her green eyes filled with secrets. They might have petted her and taken her home, but they were on their way to school. If you were late for the 8:55 bell, you had to bring a note to the principal's office and they had no note. Lizzy thought that looking into Habitat's green-for-go eyes was like looking past the lamppost into the beginning of the land of Narnia. After, they argued a lot about whether the cat had really been Habitat, but they both wanted to believe it was. They remembered how only the children in the Narnia books who believed in Narnia were rewarded and allowed to go back. Good, sensible children don't miss out by refusing to believe. But this morning in early June they saw no cats and had to run screaming down the last twenty metres of the Witchy Path because some grade six boys emerged from the bushes, pretending to be Viet Cong.

AFTER SCHOOL, Karl, Sarah and Lizzy came home to empty garbage bins and a locked house. When school started, Dad got a house key made for Karl, but Karl had forgotten it, so they waited in the garage for Dad and Wendy to come home. It was mid-November, and uncomfortable, but not unbearably cold. While they were at school, someone had taken several glass objects and hurled them against the garage two-by-fours. There were shards of orange, yellow, green and clear glass everywhere.

Everyone's fingers and toes were getting numb. They stomped around the garage, kicking bits of glass. "Watch out," Karl said. "It could land in your eye and make you blind." But they didn't stop moving or kicking. Lizzy expected Karl to make a game of it somehow—who can kick the most pieces or kick the farthest—but he didn't. He just kept kicking and stomping. His cheeks were red, and his bottom lip was sticking out in a foolish way. Lizzy wanted to console him, to touch him in some gentle way, but she knew he would pummel her if she tried.

When Dad and Wendy came home, Dad was not angry because Wendy was there with him. He was so in love that he couldn't be angry around her. Perhaps he was so in love that he must be angry when she was gone, even for a few hours, to attend a class or visit a friend.

Wendy brought leftovers from her mother's house, and they ate cottage-cheese pie with blueberry sauce for dinner. Dad and Wendy drank wine from Royal Doulton crystal wineglasses bought that afternoon to replace the thick, sea-green ones Mom had made. Wendy showed Sarah and Lizzy how to run a wet finger on the rim of a glass and make it sing. She let them dip their fingers in her wineglass and try it themselves. They were impatient about taking turns. Dad said he would give Lizzy and Sarah their own keys soon so no one would have to wait in the freezing cold garage again. He said their mother, who was living in B.C. now, trying to establish herself as a glass-blower, was coming to visit and they would work out this "custody business." Karl pushed his chair back and said he was going upstairs. Lizzy wondered if "custody" was good, bad or indifferent. Maybe it was food. Tomorrow she might ask if Mom could stay in Sarah's and her room with them when she came. She would argue that she was old enough for slumber parties. Sarah slept over at Katie's all the time anyway. Dad got up and started to clear the table. The new glass was still singing.

More, Mommy, More

Paul was thirty-six years old and a published poet. He taught English at United College. He was in his office thinking about these facts, and misery was welling up inside him. He was hot and sweating and wanted to get sick, to purge himself of himself. The sixties were over and done with, but, unlike Paul's bearded, shaggy-haired Canadian colleagues, he had actually been there. He'd been in Berkeley in 1958. He'd been in Santa Barbara when they burned down the Bank of America. He had been offered LSD by Timothy Leary himself. He had used drugs as a way of experimenting, as way of living in poetry, not because it was a trendy way to get wasted. Yet, here he was in 1971, in Winnipeg, Canada, indistinguishable from his Canadian colleagues as well as the Florida and New Jersey imports. He was one of them. What did it matter that once he had not only been on the verge of a personal vision, but had also been one of the founding members of the new American Dream? His mother had taught him one value—self-control—and he had rejected it outright. He had done peyote on the beach at three a.m. He had swum in the nude. Yet he had accomplished nothing. Soon it would be noon, and time to eat lunch in the cafeteria with Walter and Andrew.

They would discuss recent Blake criticism and how cold it was outside. He was one of them.

TEACHING WAS SOMETHING Paul had to do. It distracted him from his real work, writing poems, and he resented it. He liked to look out the window while he was lecturing and play "Naked-in-Reverse," otherwise known as "Professor Goes Berserk." The game consisted of imagining that what was naked was not, and vice versa. The trees, dry and bare in the January cold, appeared to him lush and green and with buds about to burst into blossoms. The students, bundled up in parkas and ski clothes, their heads bent as they fought the wind, were suddenly free of the confines of cold or clothing. He choreographed the dance of joy they might perform for him as they discovered, through the power of his imagination, what it was to move in a world without harshness or cold.

He didn't notice her at first. Wendy was in his Introduction to Literature class. She had knock-out, untamed auburn hair, but she was so small and still that she might have been concentrating on making herself invisible. After the first class, she came to his office to ask for additional reading. This was a classic "suck-up" tactic.

"That one lecture was worth the whole year's tuition," Wendy said. "Really. I really learned a lot."

"Maybe I should cancel the rest of the term's lectures," Paul said. "Quit while I'm ahead."

"Oh, I didn't mean that," she said. She looked genuinely flustered. She was fragile, and he was being careless with her. To make up for it, he loaned her his copy of e.e. cummings's collected poems. As a rule, he never loaned students his books, but this was a spontaneous gesture. It worked.

"You have to be brave enough to face poetry head on," he said.

"Wow. I'll bring it back next week. I promise." The book disappeared into her knapsack, and she disappeared into the mass of students moving between classes in the hallway.

After she left, he tried to say "wow" in the authentic way she had said it. "Wow... Wahow... WOW." Stupid. If anyone heard him, he would have said he was barking like a dog as an empathy exercise.

Paul was embarrassed and decided to play "disconnection." He put his head on his desk and felt the cool surface against his skin. He moved his tongue around inside his mouth, exploring his teeth and his palate. He compared the hardness of the cheek that rested on the desktop with the malleability of the other one. He rolled his tongue to produce saliva and then swallowed, then repeated the process, maintaining a rhythmic control over the amount of moisture in the environment. The world inside his mouth was real, but not comforting. He could not remember being connected to an external world. He heard students still moving and talking in the hall, but he could not decipher the sounds they made. He tried to remember the faces of his children, but they were a blur to him. Usually "disconnection," his version of meditation, was calming and sometimes even exhilarating, but this time it wasn't working. He looked up at the black-and-white photo of his daughter Sarah on the wall next to the window. She had scraggly ponytails and was wearing a boy's plaid shirt. The dirt or chocolate on her face looked like shadows. Her big eyes stared at him without shyness or camera-consciousness. It was a cute picture of a feminine little girl looking boyish. The eyes continued to stare. He remembered them as blinding white spots on the negative in the enlarger in his darkroom and looked away. He loved his children, but even as still life, they could not comfort him.

Paul thought of everything he could remember about Wendy. Why was it that the details of other people, no matter how recently they had brushed against you, were always frustratingly scant? She was small. She had amazing hair. Her fingers were white. She was able to laugh and talk at the same time. She laughed most of the time. Maybe she was nervous. Maybe he mattered to her. He thought of his wife, sad-eyed Sally. In his mind, she was permanently in rubber gloves, scrubbing burnt chicken drippings off a roasting pan that had never looked brand new. She was always crying. It was her special gift. The dishwater would be tepid and salty from her tears. He shuddered with hatred for her, or maybe he was trembling with love for Wendy. Dark, sad, Sally. Light, lilting, Wendy. Night and day. Life and death. There was something he had to do.

Yet he did nothing. He didn't even write a poem. He went home and beat his son Karl in a chess match. He ate chicken à la king with his family and avoided Sally's eyes, not because he felt ashamed, but because he hated them. The irises were a watery green that held no irony. They were animal eyes, and if he looked at them, they would claw at him. Sally was preoccupied with serving dinner. She was trying to fend off Sarah and Lizzy, who had birthdays coming up and were begging for Barbies. "Not in this house," she said, as if the dolls were devil spawn.

"But Mom, it's my birthday. And I don't even care if Lizzy gets one for her birthday too."

"I said no and I meant no," she said, her voice shaky from the effort to hold her ground. "When you're eighteen, you can have all the Barbies you want. Now just eat."

Paul knew, without looking, that there were tears forming in Sally's eyes. The girls continued to whine until, without warning, Sally lashed out at Paul. "Thanks for backing me up, Paul. United front. Thanks for all your support." Now she was really crying, but silently, and wiping her eyes with a paper towel that had already been used to clean up Lizzy's slopped à la king sauce.

"Oh, for christsakes," Paul said, choosing for private

irony his father's and grandfather's phrases, "can't we just eat in peace?"

Sarah and Lizzy were quiet now, feeling that they had once again caused their parents to turn on each other. They were comfortable with, and maybe even addicted to, mother/daughter tension, but mother/father tension made them sick with terror. It was not violence they feared, but annihilation. When Mom and Dad were fighting, the children were invisible to them, and temporarily orphaned in the house of un-love, where no one could ever care about anyone else again.

Karl had the chess board next to his plate and was quietly letting white crush black. There was a tiny click and thump as the white queen edged a black knight off the board.

PAUL WAS BLESSED with the inability to see himself in other people. He was able to read Richard Yates and John Updike stories about male despair, failed marriages and affairs with younger women without feeling humiliated. He reread *Lolita*, because it was a way of thinking about Wendy, not himself. Humbert was a small-minded loser, and Paul could not identify with him at all. Of himself he thought, I must be courageous. I must be strong. I love. I am in love. I must act. Yet for several months, nothing happened. No poetry, no kiss, no confession.

She came to his class twice a week and visited his office on the other three weekdays, usually with some burning literary question. She was not just his muse; the urgency behind her question about a particular line or image in a poem reminded him of his own long-buried authentic responses to poetry. When he talked with her, he felt like the poet Mark Strand: "Ink runs from the corners of my mouth. / There is no happiness like mine. / I have been eating poetry. . . . [The librarian] does not understand.

When I get on my knees and lick her hand / she screams. / I am a new man. / I snarl at her and bark. / I romp with joy in the bookish dark." On the weekends, Wendy disappeared completely.

As the semester drew to a close, Paul became more and more fixated on Wendy. Classes he used to dismiss early now ran twenty minutes overtime, as he struggled to find the right closing image or phrase that would make him worthy of her love. He was a better teacher for it, and only a few students closed their notebooks and zipped their jackets up to their chins in a not-so-subtle plea for dismissal. Most sat mesmerized, like Wendy, as though Paul's passion for a fearless response to the loss of nineteenth-century idealism in the twentieth-century American poets was a personal lust for each one of them.

By the end of the term, Paul wondered if he was going out of his mind. He was drinking large quantities of brewer's-yeast extract mixed loosely with grapefruit juice, recommended to him by Walter, who swore it kept him both young and sane. It tasted unbelievably awful, but it was startling in a way that Paul craved, and he had begun to feel irritable to the point of violence without it. He bought a gallon thermos and carried it around with him through the day so he had no need to go home for another hit. When he was home, he was barely conscious of where he was. There was less friction there now. The children seemed all of a sudden to be older and more independent. Paul was detached around them, but, because of the yeast drink, not always in a festering rage.

Sally spent more time in the basement blowing glass. She felt optimistic for the first time in her fifteen-year marriage. Life was finally becoming manageable. She and Paul would work it out, the way her own parents had. The children would grow up and have lives of their own. They owned this house with a reasonable mortgage, and had succeeded in paying off most of Paul's student-loan debt. Sally had never questioned that Paul was a real artist. He seemed calmer to her, dreamier; like a man about to come into his own.

For Sarah and Lizzy's birthday dinner they had hot dogs, potato chips and pickles. Karl could eat four or five hot dogs, and the girls would try to eat three. Since Paul had imposed a macrobiotic diet on everyone three months ago, the food in itself was enough of a birthday present. But Lizzy and Sarah each had one foot on the brand new Easy-Bake Oven on the floor between their chairs. After supper, they were going to make their own birthday cakes in it.

While Sarah and Lizzy fought over who got the chocolate-cake mix and who got vanilla, Paul found himself walking out of the house and getting in the car. He drank grapefruit juice and yeast straight from the thermos while he drove. Minutes later, he was crawling on his stomach through a wet, new spring lawn. He found a way to get through the ring of shrubbery that circled Wendy's house. Paul pressed his face against the basement window, but could see nothing. "I am a snake in the grass," he told himself. She was in there. The house surrounded her.

Paul was soaking wet and shivering enough to think about shedding his skin when light flooded the basement. He could see a beige sectional, a well-lacquered coffee table, an old combination stereo/TV, and lots of knick-knacks and oversize ashtrays. Wendy appeared, holding a diet 7-Up bottle and a bag of Nachos. She was wearing grey sweatpants and a pale pink Bugs Bunny T-shirt. She lay down on the couch and swung her legs up so her bare feet pressed against the wood panelling of the wall directly opposite Paul's window. He watched her for only one more delicate, long, tingling minute.

It took several evenings of waiting and watching in the damp grass before Paul was finally noticed. One night they were face to face at the basement window. Both were too terrified to officially initiate anything. They stared at each other. It was nothing like the childhood staring game in which the challenge was not to be the first to laugh. Neither was in the remotest danger of laughing. Love is a serious business. Later, they would argue playfully over who had cried out first. At the moment of recognition, Wendy was standing on a chair. Paul was caught on all fours, his face so close that his breath stained the glass. Wendy was not scared. For months now, everywhere she went, she imagined him silently behind her, watching her, about to reveal that his love for her not only existed, but was out of control. Seeing him face to face, she felt embarrassed, as if she had thrown open his office door and caught him grading in the nude. Paul felt what Wendy felt. Though she was the one on the inside of the glass, he felt caught or cornered. For the first time ever, he was slightly annoyed with her. She should not have looked up just yet.

Wendy opened the window, and Paul said, "I seem to have lost my keys."

Wendy struggled with the screen for a few seconds, then wriggled out the window like an eel sliding between marsh weeds and sat on the grass next to him. They spent several minutes crawling around together on the lawn, pretending to look for the keys. After a while, they stopped searching and sat still for a few minutes, not touching. The house was at the end of a cul-de-sac. There was no noise. Suddenly it became a shade darker. Wendy's father had woken up from his evening nap in front of the TV, turned off the lights upstairs and gone to bed. They seemed to be the only living beings in suburban Winnipeg. They could have done anything they liked: fucked on the lawn; showed each other their birthmarks; ripped up the grass and rubbed it in each other's faces.

"Ah, they were here all along," Paul said, pulling the keys out of his trouser pocket.

"Good," Wendy said. "I felt responsible."

"Well, then," Paul said. "Thank you."

This was a movie moment, and no reply was required. Paul disappeared into the night as though nothing at all was exactly what was supposed to happen.

PAUL ARRIVED HOME in a state of enchantment. On the drive, the mud on his clothes had dried hard against him, like a suit of armour. He felt that if he stood up completely, the spell would dissolve. He tried to maintain the sitting posture as he squirmed out of the car and inched into the house. On the way home it had seemed necessary to ride in and tell them all in a blaze of truth, but instead he found himself hunched in an imaginary driver's seat in the middle of a sleeping house. Flecks of dirt were spinning off him like New York City snow. Finally, the lower-back strain was too much, and he stood up, sending a storm of black flurries toward the living room rug.

Paul went upstairs and disposed of his clothes in the bathroom laundry chute. He put on his bathrobe and walked into Sarah and Lizzy's room. Lizzy slept with both arms around her stuffed bear and her head cradled between the wall and the mattress. Sarah was curled up tightly, and the small black ringlets around her temples glistened with the work of dreaming. Sleeping children are perfect, Paul thought; these sleeping children; my daughters. Paul felt he was seeing them for the first time. Quite by surprise, he had arrived at an infinite capacity to know them. This was the gift of Wendy's love. Soon, he would tell Sarah, Lizzy and Karl about the magic.

When Paul got into bed with Sally, she stirred and settled her back comfortably against him. At this moment, he felt something like love, even for Sally, but he hadn't showered. He was holding on to the dirt on his body from Wendy's yard as a way of maintaining the spell. He did not want to share it with Sally, though the pressure of her shoulder blades and curve of her ass electrified him.

When Paul finally slept, he dreamed of Sally, naked, bent over, vacuuming the living room rug. She was skinny, but her posture emphasized the three small rolls of skin on her abdomen—one for each pregnancy. Karl, Sarah and Lizzy were in the dream too, but they had shrunk to the size of little dolls. They were riding on the back of the vacuum cleaner, screaming with joy and terror each time their mother jerked it forward to work on another spot. Paul talked calmly, trying to explain to them all that everything had changed; that their lives would now be open and full. The roar of the machine was too loud, and Sally shouted, "I can't hear a word you're saying." To emphasize her frustration, she gave the hose a tremendous tug, and the children shrieked as the machine jerked and wrenched about. They shouted, "More, Mommy, more," while Paul realized he was frantically searching for something. Each time he reached into a pocket, he pulled out a small handful of dirt and tossed it angrily on the carpet. It seemed he had a thousand pockets to search.

"There, Mommy, there," the children cried, and Sally yanked the machine toward the new spot he had made.

"Hold on a damn minute," Paul said in his quietly enraged tone, which usually got results, but Sally and the children were helpless to alter their frantic pace, and Paul could not stop finding new pockets to empty. Paul's family moved wildly around the room, the children's big-toothed smiles swinging menacingly in and out of focus. Finally, Paul saw that he could end the game only by ridding himself of pockets. He started to undress, but that proved against the logic of the dream. In desperation, he began to rip and claw at his clothes, and after a suffocating, dreamtime eternity, achieved a small tear in the yoke of his sweater. He woke up with the sheet twisted in his hands. His knuckles were white.

In the shower, Paul knew that in the dream it had been Wendy he'd been madly searching for. He thought he remembered that there had been another doll-size person on the vacuum cleaner, perhaps seated between Karl and Lizzy, holding the collar of Lizzy's pyjamas with one hand, the other hand precariously waving a tall glass of soda pop. Wendy hadn't screamed at all. Paul let the warm force of the shower wash the dream over him. It no longer seemed clear to him when or what exactly he would tell them, but he knew that today was a day for poetry. Today he would write.

LINT PICKING

WENDY GOT A LOVE LETTER every day and it almost made lint picking bearable. At eighteen, she had finished first-year university, had her own apartment and was working for the summer at Northern Cloak, her grandfather's coat factory on Argyle Street in downtown Winnipeg. She worked with the other lint pickers every day from eight a.m. until four p.m., brushing the bits of lint from the fronts, backs and sleeves of the newly sewn wool coats. A good lint picker could do ten an hour, but Wendy, because she was new, because she was a relative who couldn't be fired, and because she was in love, managed only about five or six.

At ten a.m. Wendy was starting her tenth coat. The work was so monotonous that it opened up her mind to new but uninteresting perceptions. There was the constant buzz of the industrial sewing machines on the floor below. If she could only listen to just one machine, it would sound like the gentle repetition of a machine gun, a steady spray of one substance through another, but the room full of machines working made a deadly droning noise, without particulars. Closer to Wendy, the other lint pickers were picking and talking. They were mostly Cambodian immigrants and when they talked in their own language, the sounds orchestrated their work like the wrong jumpy piano music does a silent film. Out of their grim faces came happy, staccato sounds, while their hands jerked with automatic speed and precision on the coats. The English-speaking pickers talked less when Wendy was around. They couldn't trust her, regarding her alternately as a spy or, worse, an adolescent who, because of the lack of real hardship in her life, would never grow up. These were women who had given birth, who had escaped over oceans from wars and refugee camps, who had lost husbands and even children.

Wendy wasn't bothered by her isolation from the other workers. She was slowly picking the words of yesterday's letter off the wool coat in front of her. Paul had written to her in tiny, orange printing on the back of a postcard of Lake Superior. Each little ball of lint was a syllable or a word: "Don't - de - spair - little - one. I - miss - you - with - my - entire - being. - I - took - a - walk - got - lost - in - a - forest - in - Su - per - i - or - Na - tion - al - Park. - In - the - ab - so - lute - dark - ness - you - surround - ed - me. - I - could - have - be - lieved - in - any - thing - in - possibility. - Sorry - to - be - found - and - led - back - to - her - hysteria. - I - am - a - bad - dog - but - a - loy - al - one. - Is - mar - riage - still - union - if - it - is - bound - by - disgust? - I - love - you - Paul." She said his name, "Paul, Paul, Paul," for the last three pieces of lint. It was eleven o'clock, and she was on coat number fourteen.

In the daytime, Wendy could believe in her pretend adult life—job, apartment, cat, love. She was impressed by all the things she could do on her own.

At night it was harder to be alone. She talked to her friend Nora on the phone for an hour and a half. She listened again to Nora complain about her father and describe her first "true" one-night stand. She felt bad about the cheap sex, but not terrible. Sleeping with someone you don't like is like shopping at Supervalue—everything is there, each item in a yellow NO-NAME BRAND box, even things you could never want, but you feel numb. The frightening part is that you have to convince yourself that you want all of it. The trick is not to feel nothing, but to feel a love so all-encompassing that it is about as diluted as dishwater. Nora described it as generic human love, but she was afraid she was fulfilling her father's curse that because she had dyed her hair blonde, she was no longer a good girl, and that fear overshadowed any thoughts she might have about William.

According to Nora, William was about as appealing as a disposable diaper. He had that sickeningly sweet smell, and there was something rubbery about his skin, as though his pores didn't function properly. He was apologetic and clumsy, and kept telling her it was okay if they didn't "go all the way." She told him, "Look, what are we doing this for?" and that inexplicably clarified the situation for him. He stopped looking at her face and they "did it." Then it was about three a.m. and she stroked his hair because she could find no kind or appropriate words. Then he wanted to look at her again, as if she was the remains of what he had done, but she said, "You better drive me home now. My dad's going to kill me. He hates me because I used to be his favourite. He waits up for me, getting madder and madder, and then he explodes when I come home. I say, 'Dad, don't wait up for me if you hate me so much.'"

Wendy was sympathetic, but distracted. She felt she was beyond the good girl/bad girl dichotomy. Nora was still childishly proud of having disobeyed her parents. She even used the words "evil" and "accomplishment" to describe the incident with William. Wendy said that sleeping with William wasn't evil, just pointless. It didn't prove anything. She could have gone on, but, being in love, she felt the need to be magnanimous. She had recently stopped telling Nora everything about herself. Some secrecy seemed a condition of seriousness. Nora knew about Paul, but she didn't understand about Paul. If Wendy could explain, if Nora could understand, it would be as though Wendy and Paul existed as a category of love, and not as the thing itself in all its glorious and inexpressible separateness. Besides, being on the phone with Nora meant that if Paul was somehow able to get away and call her, he wouldn't be able to get through. The idea of his calling and not reaching her was unbearable. Still, Nora provided a kind of company, and when she hung up the phone, Wendy would be completely alone. While Nora talked, now about her father, Wendy stretched the phone cord as far as it would go and reached out and wiped the windowsill with her finger. Her finger was grey with dust, but there was a white streak on the sill. She took turns with her fingertips and her thumbs, wiping a clean line with each one. The sill was now almost clean, but there was no way to wipe her hands without putting the phone down.

When she said goodbye to Nora, it was eleven o'clock. If he called, it would be soon. Wendy lay in bed and tried to remember every incident and every nuance involving Paul. It was annoyingly easy to remember her side of things and even easier to invent what she couldn't remember, but difficult to maintain a full picture of Paul. For three months after the class she took from him ended, she had used every pretence possible to visit him in the neutral territory of his office. The door was always open, which was as it should be. Wendy wasn't in the market for giving Paul a quick prof-diddles-student fix; Paul was better than that, and Wendy needed to make herself real to him. He had grudgingly given her an A+ in his class, but surely there were others who had done as well. He had once referred to her in front of a colleague as "one of my best students," and the description had enraged her. She swore she would make her presence felt by him. She would blind him with it; she would be the centre of his life. Fuck him. Anyone could be a poet with a PhD. So what. She had to try to talk herself out of overreacting. True, she had written a good paper comparing cummings and W.C. Williams; they shared the same taste in style and sometimes content and maybe possibly he might be bored in his marriage and vaguely attracted to her. She was eighteen, after all. She was considered attractive. If he wasn't attracted to her, there must be something wrong with him, but maybe there was something wrong with him; maybe he was utterly self-sufficient and didn't need the frivolity of love. If he did like her, there was certainly something wrong with him. What was he doing spending his office hours mentally climbing into the pants of his first-year students?

They talked only about literature and Wendy's courses and academic plans. It was as though neither of them had the indignity of personal lives or desires. They kept coming back to Henry James, until she imagined James was part of a private code between them. "Have you read *What Maisie Knew (I love you)*?" he asked. Yes. Yes. Yes. He looked past her when he talked, out the open door at the poster in the hallway advertising a summer exchange program in Switzerland. She looked down, with a pasted smile widened by infuriating shyness, and memorized his shoes and the cuffs of his pants.

She hadn't had much experience with men. In high school she had "blown" Jim, a friend of her older brother's, because they had shared an interest in The Beatles that she had mistaken for love. They were downstairs in her parents' basement dancing to *The White Album* on full volume. When "Revolution" came on, he put his back to the speaker and pushed her shoulders down until she was kneeling. She made him do the unromantic unzipping part, but then none of it was romantic. It hurt her mouth and she had to concentrate on controlling her gag reflex. When she'd told Nora about it, Nora had laughed and said the description ruined the song for her. "How can you just laugh?" she asked Nora, but it was kind of funny, and that made her realize she didn't/couldn't love Jim. True love was a deadpan business. The sense of impending humiliation that is part of everything pleasurable or spontaneous in life must be banished for the magic of love to hold.

By two a.m. she was convinced he wouldn't call. Why

should he? He was with his family on a family vacation. She forced herself to imagine the five of them sleeping in their tent by some picturesque river or lake. It was comforting to think of each one in a separate, warm sleeping bag, but almost certainly, Paul and Sally were together, double-bagged in one large marriage bag. She was his wife. Only on old TV shows did husbands and wives not sleep together, no matter how incompatible or ill-fated. She forced herself to say the children's names—Karl, Sarah, Lizzy. There was no reason to think he would call. The names of his children exercised a veto over her belief in the magical power of love.

Sookie Rat

Mom came to Winnipeg for a visit. She and Dad had to work out a divorce agreement. They didn't talk to each other directly or even see each other face to face, but the visit was the mini-Olympics of their marriage. Before, losing had been a way of winning. They had competed for martyrdom and endurance badges that had never been awarded. Now, winning was everything. Karl felt the same excitement he had felt when he was five years old and Dad had broken down and bought a black-and-white television to watch the Tigers in the World Series. He hadn't understood a thing about baseball, but he felt a dread verging on nausea each time a Tiger player let a pitch go by. He was compelled to keep his eyes glued to the screen, and it seemed that every time he looked away the wrong team hit the ball. He was allowed to stay up until eleven o'clock to watch the final game, but even when the Tigers managed to win, his anxiety was so great that he couldn't enjoy the victory. He went to sleep and had one of several nightmares about being chased by tigers.

DURING THE MONTHS without Mom, Lizzy had felt their mother's absence the way an amputee imagines her lost limb (a comforting, idealized presence, just barely evading touch). Sarah had tried hard not to be aware of either missing her mother or of feeling her ghostly proximity. She had sworn Lizzy and Katie to secrecy about Wendy during school hours, even though Lizzy blew it when her teacher asked her class to draw their families and Lizzy included Mom and Wendy in the picture. Luckily, the teacher didn't ask any questions. After school, Sarah spent as much time as she was allowed to at Katie's.

When Mom was in town, Lizzy, who had always been a Mommy's girl, caught her mother's enthusiasm for her new life in B.C. She wanted to move there and start eating organic vegetables right away. She barely liked vegetables, but believed that the ones they would grow would taste better than Cracker Jacks. Sarah and Karl were not as keen. Like most children, they were constitutionally against change and they didn't want to leave their school and their friends. They listened to Dad's jokes about Mom's new tarpaper shack in the back woods, and each decided secretly that if the time came, they would refuse to go.

Mom pretended her visit was a holiday and brought presents for Lizzy, Sarah and Karl. Lizzy got a Skipper doll wearing hip-huggers and a halter top (practically a Barbie); Sarah got a nail-polish set, complete with glitter; and Karl got a chess clock and a book called *Everything You Always Wanted to Know about Growing Up But Were Afraid to Ask (for Boys Only)*, which he threw against the wall.

Dad and Wendy talked in hushed voices while Mom was in town, as if someone they both cared about was upstairs sleeping off a dangerous illness. The children sensed that much of their childhood was about to be decided: where they would live, whether they would be poor, who would have the daily label of parent, and what would become of Christmas and birthdays. They passed the days of the visit in the interminable but therefore bearable present tense of childhood. Sarah and Lizzy played; they fought; they got hungry and fed and hungry again. They were greedy for the extra little presents and treats that both Mom and Dad had to offer. Karl's spectator thrill wore thin and he retreated into homework and chess. He started helping his friend Pete with his paper route and spent a lot of time on the phone with ticket agents, finding out about special rates to New York City and San Diego. Several times a day, he calculated how many papers he still had to deliver before he could make his escape.

ONE DAY, MOM came over when Dad and Wendy were out. She only came when they were out, so her visit was loosely expected. "Bring whatever you need," she told them. "Possession is nine-tenths of the law. Come on. I'm kidnapping you."

Lizzy brought her toothbrush and, in her excitement, the top to a pair of pyjamas, but not the bottoms. Karl and Sarah were enraged by this new twist in their lives and refused to bring anything. "We don't want to be kidnapped," they said. "You can't make us."

"Do you think I have a choice?" she demanded. "I can't let him screw me out of everything."

In the car, Lizzy looked at her pyjama top and saw that it wasn't even clean. A large spaghetti-sauce stain and several smaller ones littered the front of it. Looking at her completely useless pyjama top made her inexplicably hate Karl and Sarah for not wanting to be kidnapped. Here she was, in the back seat of the car, with Mom at the wheel, taking her to somewhere new and exciting. She didn't really understand that Mom and Dad were at war, but she knew that all of a sudden, it felt like Mom might be the winner. Yet there they were, Karl and Sarah, grumpy and sullen, jammed beside her, poking her because, by definition, she took up too much room and was spoiling everything.

Mom was smoking a menthol cigarette and driving fast. Lizzy felt like they were in a movie. Last year, Mom and Dad had taken all three of them to see a university-hall screening of *Bonnie and Clyde*. They thought they were more mature than other kids, luckier too, sitting up late in the college theatre. Lizzy and Sarah had never seen people die before. They watched the blossoming massacre finale with something like detachment mixed with awe. Death, beautiful death. Machine guns like dance music. All right then. Mom and Lizzy would be Bonnie and Clyde. Karl and Sarah could be Clyde's no-good family.

When Karl wasn't fantasizing about running away, he wanted, more than life itself, to stay in Winnipeg with Dad and Wendy. They left him alone, mostly, treated him like a grown-up, and he had friends. Pete Mahichuck was his best friend, and they played hockey every day after school during the cold months. The rest of the time, they played metal hockey in Pete's rec room and ate bags of taco chips with extra-hot salsa, all provided by Pete's dull, loving, normal parents. At school, he and Pete were members of a moderately popular clique. There were more girls than boys in their group and they joked around a lot. For ninth grade, it was pretty good. They had fun. Mom wanted to take them to a hick fish farm, 2000 miles away on Vancouver Island. They would have to take a school bus. There would be no escape.

Mom brought the children to a friend's house. Sarah and Lizzy sat on the nearly new shag carpet and sorted jelly beans from a glass dish on the coffee table Mom had made. They laid them out in rows of colour: red, yellow, green, pink and the coveted black ones. Karl sat in the brown leather recliner, blasting the large colour console with the remote control. At home they had no "granddad furniture" like this chair. There was no colour TV, no cable and no remote control either. Karl switched between auto racing and *The Brady Bunch*. Would Mom find her own Mr. Brady with three or four brats of his own to fuse with Sarah, Lizzy and Karl? It was unthinkable. Karl ran through the channels twice, then found the auto racing again. He didn't care about cars, but the drone of the announcer's voice on top of the buzz of the cars was at least not grating.

"Karl, I need you in the kitchen," Mom called.

"What?" Karl moved in the chair enough to make the leather squeak, but he did not get up.

"Karl. Please." She did not use her "I'm about to lose it" voice; there was no edge of hysteria in her tone. Karl, who used to be able to tease her, laugh in her face, and then run to his room and slam the door in response to her slightest request, was compelled to obey. He walked into the kitchen, and Mom handed him the phone.

"I need you to call your father."

"Are we going home now?"

Mom maintained her Superwoman-like command over Karl. "Tell him if he won't sign the agreement, he'll never see his children again." She said "his children" as though she were talking about some found object: a meteor that landed in someone's wheat field; Baskin and Robbin's secret recipe for Rocky Road ice cream. "His children" was a valuable prize, but it did not mean Karl: his life, his school, his friends, everything that she had no right to destroy.

"Why don't you tell him?" Karl asked, but his question was more bravado than belligerence. He knew that it was impossible for her to talk to Dad and that it was cruel to even suggest it. He glared at her and dialled the phone number for home.

Karl heard Dad's steady, strong voice on the line. "Take it easy, son. Everything is fine. Are the girls with you?"

"Don't tell him where we are," Mom whispered at him, and pressed her ear against the outside of the receiver so she wouldn't miss anything.

Karl yanked his head away. "Here. We're all here. It's

just that Mom's kidnapping us, so you have to sign the agreement or ... or ..."

"Or you'll never see your children again," Mom prompted.

"Or you'll never see your children again." Karl spoke the last words quickly, like a child reciting a poem he doesn't care about and doesn't understand. He wanted Dad to understand that the phrase "your children" had no directive power over Karl.

"Just a minute, son. Can you hold the line?"

There was a long pause and Karl imagined Dad looking at his savings account passbook, or checking the cash in his wallet to see if he could afford "the agreement." Dad hated to spend money carelessly. Maybe he would bargain for only one or two of the children. Surely he could do without Lizzy, who clung to Mom like a barnacle and was too little to do anything for herself. Sarah wasn't much better, though instead of whining all day, she threw herself on the floor kicking and screaming at the slightest frustration. Karl could make Kraft dinner and Lipton's soup. "I never need a babysitter. I don't need anything. Choose me. Choose me. Oh God. Let it be me," Karl chanted silently.

Finally, Karl heard Dad's voice. "Son, I'm going to have to talk to my lawyer about this. Can I get right back to you?"

"Um..."

"Tell him he has an hour. We'll call him back in an hour," Mom instructed.

"Yeah. I'll call you back, Dad. In an hour."

"Sit tight, son."

PAUL DIDN'T NEED an hour to make up his mind. The agreement appeared more than fair. She got her share of the house when it was sold, about $10,000 dollars, and $400 a month in child support once the school year ended and the children went to live with her. If she earned any money, he would reduce his payments by 50% of whatever amount she earned over the first $100. He would be her own little welfare state, with tepid incentives built in. Paul would agree because it was worth it just to stop fighting with her. True, he didn't want to give her a cent or let her take over the children again, and if they went to court, he could argue Sally was crazy and an unfit mother. His lawyer, Wendy's brother, was pushing for that strategy. But Lizzy clearly missed her mother—she was clingy and constantly chewing on her matted split ends—and whatever happened, everyone had agreed from the start that the children should stay together. Besides, it was getting harder and harder for him and Wendy to maintain the serene bliss they shared together with the children always fighting with each other, needing something, getting colds and never cleaning up after themselves. By kidnapping his children, Sally was offering him victim status and a chance to have Wendy all to himself. When Karl called back, Paul didn't hesitate: "My God. Tell her to bring you home. Whatever she wants, I'll sign."

The children were home by bedtime. On the drive home, Mom was nervously excited about her success. She told the kids how wonderful it would be next year when they could all live together in a country house on Vancouver Island. "Can I get a horse?" Lizzy asked.

"We'll see," Mom said. "Not right away."

The older two asked for nothing, feeling that if they could just block out this future, it would not arrive.

Karl hung around downstairs after the girls had gone to bed, but Dad and Wendy were snuggling on the couch reading a Thomas Hardy novel together, and the only thing Dad said was, every few minutes, "Okay?" or "Can I turn the page now?"

"Well, goodnight," Karl said, and Dad and Wendy looked startled.

"Goodnight, son. You'll feel better about things in the

morning," Dad said, and he reached out to touch Karl's hair. Karl didn't pull away, and he stayed downstairs a few minutes longer, waiting for Dad to say, "Of course I'll let her have the girls; they're too young to be away from their mother, but we want you to stay with us." But he wasn't the kind of dad who read your mind and told you what you wanted to hear. Wendy carefully put a bookmark in the book and said, "Hey, Karl, when are you going to teach me how to play chess? I really want to learn."

"Maybe tomorrow," Karl said. He found their casual friendliness comforting, as though nothing could possibly be their fault. He wanted to believe in the world of measured voices and like minds they presented, but their voices did not offer any escape for him. He would be on his own in rural hell the day after the school year ended. So far he had only saved $25.00, and a ticket to New York City cost $412.00. He went upstairs and got Sookie, the stuffed rat he had had forever, out from under his bed. Sookie was missing an ear because after one particularly bad day in grade two, where all year at school Karl had been public enemy number one, he had gone home and bitten Sookie Rat's ear off and spat it on the floor. He tried, as he had tried on many occasions, to pull or bite the second ear off, but it was immovable. It hurt his teeth and he got nowhere. "Fuck you, Sookie Rat," he whispered, and bounced the rat across the floor.

ARRIVALS

THE BUS RIDE FROM WINNIPEG to Vancouver took thirty-four hours and twenty-five minutes. Mom and Barbara were waiting at the Vancouver bus depot for Karl, Sarah and Lizzy. Mom was still thin, and wore stylish jeans from the east with double seams of bright white stitching. Barbara was taller than Mom, and angular, with short hair that made even her face pointy. She looked brittle, half-starved and afraid. Barbara was not a talker. She stood shoulder to shoulder with Mom, even while Mom was hugging the children, to let them know that she was not "just a friend." Mom said, "Kids, this is Barbara. I love her, and I want you to love her too. We're all going to be so happy in our new life together."

Sarah said, "Hi," in an automatic way. She was blinded by the intensity of green and shocked by the west coast aroma that surrounded even the bus depot on the seamy side of downtown Vancouver. She had been too young when they'd lived in British Columbia years ago to remember anything about the look and smell of living near an ocean. She knew that buses and bus depots smelled a certain way, but she was surprised that her new life would smell like salt and fish. Winnipeg, she remembered, smelled neutral, like real life.

Karl said, "Hi, Barbie. Pleased to meet you. Where's Ken?" If he was aware that he was setting the tone for their whole relationship, he didn't care. Barbara flinched and tightened her smile. She had no experience with fifteen-year-old boys who are made of rocks and snails and puppy-dogs' tails and sarcasm. She chose a line from a fifties western she had seen on late TV sometime. "We're all gonna get along just fine, son. You wait and see," she said, still sleeve to sleeve with Sally.

"I want to go on the boat," Lizzy said. At last their boxes and bags were released from the compartments underneath the bus seats, and everyone got to carry something to the van. Barbara drove to the B.C. Ferries terminal in Horseshoe Bay in the 1967 blue Chevy Van with no windows in the back—Mom and Barbara's first joint purchase. Karl, Sarah and Lizzy leaned against their sleeping bags on an old mattress and felt the road vibrating through them. Mom told them about the neighbourhood children—a girl Karl's age, a boy between Karl and Sarah's age, and two girls down the road Lizzy's age.

"What about me?" Sarah demanded.

"I'm sure there will be somebody your age around," Mom said. "Anyway, there is the ocean and the woods, and you have Lizzy to play with."

"I don't care," Sarah said. "I have friends at home."

"Let's try to be positive," Mom said. "This is a new start for everyone."

There was a long wait at the ferry dock, then it got dark inside the van as they idled in the belly of the boat, waiting for the signal to climb the metal stairs to the passenger levels of the ferry.

BARBARA DROVE THE van from the B.C. ferry terminal in Nanaimo to their new home in Qualicum Bay. Mom was happy, playing the tour guide, providing details about the little towns they passed along the way. Qualicum Bay was about an hour from Nanaimo. "This is Parksville. It's really just a tourist town. Here is Qualicum Beach, not Qualicum Bay. There's your school, Karl. There is the bakery and the library and the Quality Mart. Of course we joined the food co-op in Coombs, but that's inland a few miles." In B.C., Mom had undergone some sort of conversion that centred around organic food and suspicion of products in brightly coloured packages. The new God was anything that could be defined as "natural."

Karl and Sarah sat up on the hood of the motor, just behind the front seats, watching the trees, trailer parks and other buildings go by. Sometimes they could see the ocean, but mostly they saw the deep green of the fir trees that lined the Island Highway. Lizzy lay down in the back. She had taken Yum Yum, the life-size bear Mom had made for her ages ago out of Karl's old fake-fur parka, out of her box and hugged him to her chest. She didn't want to have names and specifics attached to their new life just yet. Lying on the mattress, she could look up and see her brother, her sister, her mother, and, through the windshield, the blinding green of B.C. woodlands. Except for the rainbow-coloured baseball cap, she could see nothing of Barbara. She heard Mom saying, "Here is where you'll catch your school bus. This is our road. It's really just a logging road...."

Mom made it sound like the island was enchanted, like there was no anger here, no possibility of loss. This was because living in the country meant they would get to eat "real food," which they would grow themselves. Karl and Sarah had been watching every break in the green for a glimpse of the ocean, the way a soothsayer watches for a hopeful sign. They tried to decipher every billboard, telephone pole and building they passed. They refused to take Mom's word for anything, but Lizzy, on the mattress in the back, with her face rubbing the flat, wide cheek of her stuffed bear, smelled his "I'll always be your bear" smell and found herself almost believing she had arrived. It was amazing that her mother and Barbara could rescue her from her whole life, when no one had ever even told her she had been in prison. She was trying to believe it, but maybe her heart wasn't pure. She liked junk food, even if she didn't worship at the shrine of McDonald's the way Karl did. Maybe garden vegetables would put an end to pain and conflict. It was as if the whole bus ride and now here in the back of the van were the hushed birthday-party moment when you cover your eyes and grin and fidget, waiting for them to bring you that wonderful present that is too large and strange to wrap. Lizzy thought it might be fine to wait forever to open her eyes. Then Barbara drove the van up the winding driveway, and they were home.

Karl went right into the house, ignoring Mom's cry to come and see the tomatoes which were almost ripe in the back garden. He wanted to know if the house had running water. Amazingly, there was a real bathroom, though the fixtures were ancient and rusty. The tile might have once been green, but was crumbling and black now. Karl tried to close the door to the bathroom. There was a grey, plastic sliding door with a leather strap with a hole in it which fit over a nail on the door frame. No matter how much he pulled the door, he couldn't get it to close all the way. There was always a space of an inch or two. He tried to be relieved that there was running water, but the water that limped out of the tap had a rusty tinge. His mother had promised fresh artesian spring water, and his father had jokingly called him and Sarah, Jack and Jill. He had envisioned a wooden washtub in the middle of the kitchen with himself and Sarah in lederhosen and bright red cheeks bringing buckets of water from a picturesque little wishing well. He would have thrown himself into the well—anyone would have. This bathroom was better than an outhouse with a lucky horseshoe nailed above the door and a gaping stink hole inside like the ones remembered from so many family camping trips, but it was still awful. Karl was glad he had no friends in their new neighbourhood who might come over and ridicule the house. He didn't plan on making any, either.

Lizzy and Sarah looked at the garden. There were cabbages and leaf lettuce, tomatoes, carrots and beans. There was also a strawberry patch with little white strawberries that Barbara said would be ripe in a few weeks. Lizzy and Sarah looked at Barbara when she said this. It was the first thing she'd said since greeting the children at the Vancouver bus depot. Hearing Barbara's enthusiasm made both girls want to find a way to get all the strawberries for themselves, even if it meant working together.

"Can we have the strawberry patch for our garden?" Lizzy asked. "We'll weed it ourselves."

"Barbara's done a lot of work on it already," Mom said. "Anyway, there'll be enough for everyone."

AFTER A YEAR in beautiful British Columbia, Lizzy was still pining to see her mother again, even though they were all living together now in the house Mom called "her own place" and Karl called a stinking tarpaper shack. Lizzy was still waiting for the perfect reunion she had anticipated so fiercely that whole year of living with Dad and Wendy. When she thought about Mom, she still felt a yearning and loyalty so strong it manifested itself as nausea. The difference was that now Mom was there, always trying to get her to eat some kitchen-sink soup or lentil casserole. Lizzy tried to like the health food Mom was so thrilled with, but she had never had much of an appetite for anything other than fruit and cinnamon toast. She ate like a feeble little sparrow, picking and moving the food around on her plate. When Barbara said, "If that girl doesn't eat a little more, she's going to dry up and blow away in the wind," Mom looked crushed, like Lizzy was deliberately trying to starve herself to death as a way of undermining the tiny bit of happiness Mom and Barbara had carved out for themselves.

SARAH, WHO WAS now eleven, had a best friend, Chrissy, who lived in Bowser close to the elementary school, and when Sarah wasn't at her house, they were talking on the phone. She and Chrissy modelled themselves on Nancy Drew and tried to appear clean, pretty and competent. They were convincingly normal. Sarah seemed to believe that if she got the normal pose exactly right, it would act as a kind of coercive magic and she would wake up one morning to find that her house and family had been transformed into the Waltons or the Brady Bunch. When other kids at school said things to her like, "Are you a lezbo like your mom?" she smiled primly and made herself believe in the magic even more intensely. Unlike Karl or the old Winnipeg Sarah, she never said "fuck you" or threw herself on the ground in a fit when other kids jeered about Mom and Barbara. She had learned from television dramas and teen fiction that *everything* works out for promising, shiny-faced, polite, shy, yearning young girls like Chrissy. Their taunts were a test—if she didn't react to them, she passed.

At home, Sarah found she and Barbara could easily avoid each other. Effortlessly, they developed a relationship where words were never directly exchanged. It was simpler to go without than to make the concession of asking Barbara to pass the salt.

KARL RELIGIOUSLY NURTURED an atmosphere of rage and hatred regarding Barbara. Except for intermittent shouting matches, they ignored each other, but took every opportunity to plead their side to Mom.

"Mom, why doesn't she get a job so we don't have to live like this?"

"Karl is old enough to help out in the garden. When I was a kid I had chores. Why do you let him walk all over you?"

"Mom, why do you let her turn us into a freak show? At least Dad married someone normal. She doesn't belong here. She's a waste of human space."

"Are you really going to drive him into town for that party tonight? I just don't know what we'd do if the van broke down."

"I hate that fucking bitch and I hate you." And then, to Barbara, the only words he'd directly spoken to her in several months, "I hate you, you fucking sponger. Get a job. We don't need any leeches around here." Karl was denied the dignity of slamming the door to his room. He shoved the grey plastic slider across the doorway. It hit the door frame and bounced back an inch or two. He lay on his bed and the sounds of his sobbing filled the house. After a while, there were a few minutes of quiet while Karl plugged his electric guitar into the $18.00 amp he'd bought with his own money, left over from his paper-route days in Winnipeg. He played one long solo—maybe forty-five minutes of tortured, inhuman sounds. The house resonated with his rage long after it was spent and he was asleep in his clothes, with one arm around the guitar and the light still on in his room.

Mom looked in, but didn't risk taking the guitar away or covering him with a blanket. My baby's so grown up, she thought. He'll have to make his own way, somehow. She remembered when he was little and asked if he could bring his tiggy-piggy blanket to Heaven. "Yes, of course," she'd said, though she and Paul had agreed to raise the children as atheists and not be afraid to tell them the truth about everything.

She went into the living room and sat down close to Barbara, who was reading *The Whole Earth Catalogue* on the couch. She wanted to tell her that Karl didn't mean those things he said. That he was just a scared, angry kid; that it was her fault for not being firm with him when he was smaller. But she was afraid to have Barbara think about her kids too much. It wasn't fair to her, and she was afraid Barbara would get sick of the whole thing and opt out. Instead they talked about the garden and the plans for the glass-blowing studio. The salmon would be spawning soon and they could load up the van with free fertilizer (dead fish, covered in white fungus and washed up on the shore for one and all) and dig it into the garden. When the weather turned colder, they would get to work insulating the studio.

Barbara put her arm around Mom and rubbed her cheek on her shoulder. Mom snuggled closer and felt a warm, secure overflowing of love and gratitude. Barbara had been willing to give up everything—college, life on the ranch with her parents, a good job at an arts-supply store—so that they could start a life together. Mom and Barbara didn't care about money or status. They were partners in love, in the glass-blowing business and in their lifestyle of choice. They were together. The children would grow up and find their own way to be happy, whether they liked organic vegetables and sewing their own clothes or not. They were smart like their father and resourceful like their mother. It was only because they were children that they hated change so. In time they would see that with Barbara's help, Mom had done what was best for them. In time.

But Not Yet

Sooner or later
we must come to the end
of striving

to re-establish
the image the image of
the rose

but not yet
you say extending the
time indefinitely

by
your love until...

—William Carlos Williams
(from "The Rewaking")

I WAS BORN ON THE PEACE BRIDGE between Buffalo and Fort Erie in a taxi that contained my father, my mother, my brother Karl, my sister Sarah, the driver and a large St. Bernard dog we had picked up as a stray a few days earlier in Delaware Park. According to family legend, we were speeding toward the Canadian side, where we could avoid the nightmare of American health-care costs, when I found my way into the world. Apparently, the driver demanded compensation for stained leather seats. My father argued that the damage was an act of God and therefore he was not responsible, but he gave him twelve American one-dollar bills in lieu of a cigar, when he dumped us all off at the Queen Elizabeth Hospital. The meter read only $10.75.

Since that spring day in 1963, I had always preferred "between" to "here" or "there." That is, until recently, when I thought I had arrived at a comfortable, adult place. I live alone in Montreal. I write for the *Montreal Mirror*, that true north hip and free publication that tells English Montrealers which clubs are worth standing in line for each week. I just got back from a purely pleasure trip to Paris, financed by student-loan money and rebates from the courses I'd dropped at Concordia University. I'd stayed for free in a loft above an English bookstore in Paris appropriately called "Shakespeare's," lived on baguette and Camembert and wrote letters every afternoon from the courtyard of the Rodin Museum. At night, I snuck a copy of William Carlos Williams's collected poems out of the bookstore, up to my loft, and memorized the verses that seemed necessary not just to read but to incorporate into my every breath, my every movement and even into my dream life. Paris was a bit lonely and reserved, but otherwise the perfect adventure for an independent eighties girl with no strings attached. Right?

IT HAS BEEN almost a year since I left the love of my life because I didn't want him to kill me. He had come close, but I saw myself as a survivor, not a victim, as the cliché goes. Our last fight was about who would make the pancake batter into pancakes while I was on the phone long distance with my sister. True, it was something I usually did as part of my whining bribery campaign to convince him that I wasn't his enemy. But the phone was in the other room, and she had called, and when I told her it was a bad time, she said, as though Geoff and I were a normal couple like she and Eric, or Rosanne and Dan Arnold, "Tell him to make his own stupid pancakes. You're talking to your sister long distance." Just her saying it made it obvious that I was a total pushover if I didn't demand that he finish making the pancakes, but that demand was completely outside the logic of our relationship.

After a while, I heard him crashing around the kitchen, and then the back door slammed. When I got off the phone, there were half-baked, gooey messes in the frying pan and some dishes were smashed on the floor, along with the syrup bottle. Maple-flavoured syrup was oozing along the linoleum and spreading in a wide arc under the stove. I knew that if I stayed, he would be home in a few hours so we could scream at each other between pleading for absolution. The climax might be Geoff running off into the night in only socks and jeans and me running after him, calling his name, really believing he might die of exposure or worse. He would be a few blocks toward the mountain, far enough for me to prove something by finding him. He would step out from behind a tree and say, "Baby. Oh, Baby. Let's never hurt each other again." He would see that I had matched his love and topped it by chasing his sock prints in bare foot prints in the snow. He was strong (he used to play football) and he would pick me up and carry me all the way home, and I would feel the inclusive, mummifying love a baby has for its mother. He would carry me up the stairs and put me on the bed on my back. He would kneel beside the bed, take off my jeans and rub my toes until they were tingling with life again. I would lie still, thinking that it would be so perfect if this time he would literally fuck me to death; that's how in love we were. The mess in the kitchen would never be spoken of again.

But the next day there would be something else.

Sarah's phone call violated the privacy necessary for Geoff and I to keep at each other the way we did. My sister's matter-of-fact voice had severed that suicide logic. I stayed with Geoff one more week, lying and smiling and imagining myself as other. It's interesting how easy it is to lie when you're afraid the truth will get your head bashed against a chimney. Anyway, I was in the habit of placating.

All week we were cool and rational with each other. When he left for pick-up basketball on Friday afternoon, I packed some clothes and favourite books and went to stay at the YWCA until I could get a place. I was terrified that he would find me, and he did, but he was the politest of stalkers, sending a dozen baby white roses, a few poems, then nothing.

A FEW DAYS later, I moved into this apartment. It's a two-and-a-half on St. Dominique Street just north of Rachel Street in the part of Montreal that is Portuguese, English and French. It's on the second floor with a big picture window in the main room, which overlooks the textiles factory across the street. The main room is divided into a sleeping room and a living room space, with a cute half-wall between the two. I had just enough furniture: a mattress, a dresser, a sofa, a rug, a kitchen table and three chairs. On one wall I have a way-larger-than-life-size poster of Sandrine Bonnaire from *Sans toi ni loi*. It doesn't sound like much, but as the victim-turned-survivor line goes, it was mine; it was my point of arrival. I'd lived here for over eleven months. I still thought about Geoff, but mostly as the wilderness I had passed through. The operative words were "passed through"—I was now on the other side. I had a job and friends, and people told me often that I was clever and skinny and even admirable.

WHEN I GOT off the plane from Paris, I was in a zombie-like state of fatigue. I took a taxi home. In the past, when David had stayed in my apartment, he always left before I got back. I would put my key in the lock—click, click—and there was my place, exactly as I had left it, except maybe a little cleaner. I had never before found it ominous that there were absolutely no traces of David's presence when I returned home. Not one cigarette butt. Not one lost sock. No leftover food items or used can of shaving cream in the bathroom garbage. No David smell, no sign of David at all. But it was strange. It was as though when he entered my world he tried to erase himself and become me. How flattering.

Other times, when we saw each other after he'd stayed in my place, he would always have read two or three of my books, and we would talk about them. It's nice to have friends who love what you love. I just didn't know that meant he would have to be annihilated. I should have known. I'd spent most of my life begging people to help me annihilate myself in exchange for just a tiny minute of belonging with them. But, supposedly, I was over that.

David was my friend because he was from the outside. He was actually from Iraq. His parents had left him there when he was two so they could come to Canada and start a better life for him. By the time he was old enough to travel by himself and come and join them, he had two younger siblings who spoke English and recognized their parents' faces. They are both American heart specialists now, but David is still missing in action; not living the sort of life his parents sacrificed everything for, including him. I knew about his past, but I thought he had survived it. I knew his parents wanted him to be a brain surgeon, but I thought he was happy being like me. We were individuals. People who had choices and chose trendy austerity over ambition. I didn't expect us to get older or intimate or have breakdowns. I thought we had arrived in a bearable present tense.

This time, the apartment was not at all as I had left it. All my furniture was gone. He must have sold it or maybe he just called the Goodwill and invited them to take it all away. Even my books and clothes were gone. There was no food in the cupboards. The fridge was bare except for three or four dairy creamers and some packets of catsup. There was no toothpaste and no toilet paper in the bathroom. The bathtub was encrusted with a ring of filth as thick and as textured as a Van Gogh canvas. Everything that was moveable had been removed except for Sandrine Bonnaire, whose inscrutable three-foot face was exactly the kind of mirror I didn't want.

I put my suitcase down on the floor and sat on it. I tried to do something normal and leafed through the mail that had accumulated while I was away. Thankfully, I had forgotten to give David the key to the mailbox or he might have sold my mail for kindling or done to it whatever he did with the rest of my life. There was a free credit-card offer from Canadian Tire, the phone bill, a letter from Wendy, my ex-stepmother, a postcard from my sister with a Degas dancer on the front and on the back, in her precise, no-problems printing,

> *Hi Sis,*
> *Remember me? It's been forever since we've seen you. Please write.*
> *Love,*
> *Sarah*

There was also a letter from Mary-Jane. She was my mom's next-door neighbour when I was nine years old and I moved in with my mom on Vancouver Island after a long year of living in Winnipeg with my dad and his second wife, Wendy. Mary-Jane is a flower child, earth mother, born-again type with a brood of her own blonde-haired precocious children. When I met her, I recognized her as the perfect replica of the mother I had invented and pined for that whole aching year of living with my dad. When I was eleven, Mary-Jane baptized me herself in the salt waters of Qualicum Bay. I held my body like a two-by-four, and she dipped it straight back, under and straight up again. For a little girl who was petrified of getting water in her eyes, even when she dropped her head back into the bathtub to wash her hair, the baptism was a kind of washing away of fear. In my eleven-year-old logic, Mary-Jane was my saviour. Everything I imagined about God, I imagined through her blonde, wispy, laughing, loving presence. She never yelled at her kids. She even played with them. She let them get covered with mud in her garden and she nursed each of them until they were three years old and she was pregnant with the next one. She never asked me to leave her house. I loved her. Because my family was vaguely Jewish, I felt guilty about the Christ element of her religion, but for a time, I loved her enough to believe it all.

A few months before I went to France, I had written her to explain the state of my soul and thereby test her love for me. I wanted hers to be the greatest, truest love. I was afraid she could only love children who loved God; and I was now a full-grown sceptic. Having inadvertently grown up and misplaced my faith, I feared I was lost to her, but I figured I was old enough to take it. I told her that I had trouble with the Christ-is-the-one-and-only-one bit and that left me with God. Then I told her that I was with Ivan in *The Brothers Karamazov*: God or no, I choose *not* to believe, thank you very much. Sorry. And do you still love me? Because if you aren't God enough to love me in spite of everything, in spite of the fact that I don't believe in you, then why bother? Even now, even though more than ten years ago, when I was thirteen, I had left Mom and Mary-Jane and moved back to my Dad and Wendy's place in Winnipeg, Mary-Jane was still my image of God. I wanted to shake it, but I needed her divine love anyway. The letter from Mary-Jane was short:

Dear Lizzy:

You are a lamb who has strayed from the flock. There were many temptations along the way. I pray that you will come back and follow the one true God, our Lord and Saviour, Jesus Christ.

Rachel is living on her own in town now. We get along better. Jonas is growing up to be a fine young man. He still goes to school and plays guitar in a band. Avery is still my little angel and Daniel and Aaron are so grown up you wouldn't know them.

Sammy and I still talk about moving the family back east, although there isn't much work there and Rachel might stay behind. At least Sammy is working now, praise God.

My home is with Jesus. Won't you come home too, my wild pony?

God Bless,
Mary-Jane

I sat on my suitcase and cried. Maybe she had never loved me. Maybe she just wanted to arrive in Heaven with a big list of converts to flash at St. Pete. But wasn't I just trying to convert her? I told myself no. I wanted her to love me in spite of our difference, that's all.

I remembered the time we were driving into town in her 1968 pickup truck. She was driving and nursing the baby, Avery, at the same time. Next to her was Jonas, age four, and on my lap was Rachel, age eight. Rachel had decided she was a cat about two months earlier and refused to say anything except "meow" for no and "meow meow" for yes. She was comfortable on my lap, hissing and scratching at Jonas. At that time, the Island Highway was a fairly narrow and winding two-lane road. A logging truck was barrelling towards us, relatively safe in its own lane, but a large branch was working its way loose from the truck's load and was directly in our path at the moment we rounded the corner and faced the truck. There was no time to react. In the seconds before the branch would have reached us, probably smashing us all to hell, it slipped down a few more feet. The branch swiped the side mirror and turned it completely around, but we were not even hurt. Mary-Jane had a voice that was always melodic and light, never harsh or grating. "Thanks, God!" she sang out, and we went on to buy cookies at the bakery in town as if it were unremarkable that we were God's children, perfectly protected from harm.

Rereading her letter, I wanted to hurt her—to take her by her blonde ponytail and make her look into my eyes until she said she understood me. I wanted to rip out all the pages in *The Brothers Karamazov* and make her eat them one by one. I remembered that she was four thousand miles away and just someone who had been kind to me for a time because I had been a needy little girl who needed a surrogate home.

I still had my ex-stepmother's letter in my hand but was afraid to open it. Like Mary-Jane, she had not written to me in several years. It felt like Judgement Day. Wendy's version of reality was always so much more coercive than everyone else's.

> *Dear Lizzy:*
> *Yes, indeed. A letter from me at long last. Are you dumbfounded? I miss you. There is a hole in my life here in Winnipeg without you. Nikko misses you too. I am practicing now at the St. James Clinic. It is a real bore—thirty percent non-specific vaginal itch, thirty percent snotty-nosed kids and forty percent lonely old fogeys on a pile of meds. I thought being a doctor was supposed to be glamourous.*

Anyway, things are really falling apart here. I am trying to hold this joint-custody thing together, but, as usual, your Dad is being a real prick about it. He will take Nikko away from me if he can. He is that spiteful. That's why I'm writing you. I need you to come home and help me save my son's childhood. If you could just come for the summer, you could stay with us and look after Nikko while I'm at work. I know you're on my side, but if you were physically here, looking after Nikko, Andy [her brother the lawyer] says our case would be cinched. Gabe has moved out, at least temporarily, until he can get the boozing thing under control. Some days I think it's just hopeless. Some days I wish he would just finish himself off, but there are good days too.

So, here is my life, disaster that it is. I remember the great times we had together, and I want Nikko to have that sense of family. How are things with you? Of course you need time to think about this. Please let me know soon though as I will have to clean out the study for you. The court date is in September, so obviously, the sooner you could come and the longer you could stay, the better.

With Love,
Wendy

I sat there trembling with rage or some deeper unnameable emotion. What madness possessed me to open the phone bill? I guess I was still trying to find a normalizing activity; something to give me my world back. The phone bill was a fat, five-page listing of calls to Baghdad, Halifax and San Luis Obisbo. The total was

$1875.00. I didn't know where David was or why he would do this to me. There was no way I could pay this kind of bill. I had heard about the collection police in Quebec who go under cover, follow people around, sometimes even into their beds, and then snatch whatever they can: TVs, family heirlooms, even bicycles. I had none of these things, but David's global phone chats ruled out the possibility that I ever would. The only explanation was that he had gone crazy. I remembered an anecdote he told me once about how he had been hit by a car, lost his memory and spent six months in a mental hospital. It had seemed pretty fantastic for meek, solicitous David, but it made me respect him too. There was suffering mixed with his trendy austerity, and it gave him depth, but I was furious at him for doing his craziness to me. It wasn't until three days later, when I confronted him in the chess club, that it sunk in how lost he was.

"IT'S US AND THEM," he told me. He was trembling and sweating. He was dressed in my mauve cotton guru pants and my "Our Town" T-shirt. Clearly he had been wearing these clothes for several days, maybe even weeks. He'd been slight before, but now he must have lost fifteen or twenty pounds. "It's us and them. I thought you were us, but you're them."

"Look David, just tell me what's wrong. I want to help. I do."

"You're wrong. You're deranged, that's all."

I held up the $1875.00 phone bill. "David, I trusted you. Who is going to pay this?"

He started to convulse with sobs. He pushed his body further into the space between the sofa and the wall. Even though it took me three days to track him to the chess club office and we were finally face to face, he still believed it was possible to hide from me. He was crying like a little boy, but his words, though hard to decipher through the sobbing, had adult-strength venom. "Bitch. You think you're so fucking out there. Confrontation model psychology. Go fuck yourself, fucking bitch. I don't need you. You think you know something about me. Yeah? You know sacred cow shit. Them. Them. Don't need no them." He took to this last line and started repeating it over and over like a mantra.

"Hey, David, it's me, Lizzy. It's okay. We're friends, remember? We used to walk all over Montreal arguing about existentialism. Remember? We'd go for coffee at two in the morning. You are the only guy in this city I trust. Remember? I told you that. I told you that a hundred times."

"Them. Them. Don't need no them. Don't need no them."

"David, please. Let's go get something to eat. Let's get through this together. Doesn't our friendship matter to you?" But I was thinking that I just wanted to get away from him. The trust I was talking about had completely evaporated three days ago when I'd arrived home from my first-ever European vacation.

"Them. Them. Them is you," he was still chanting and building a small supply of spittle around the corner of his mouth. Obviously I couldn't reason with him at all. He was too far gone, but I was losing it too. There was barely a thread of compassion in my anger at him. My "Our Town" shirt clung to his bony shoulders, and the fabric was thin enough that you could almost count his ribs through it. My guru pants had dark sweat patches along his thighs. I kept thinking that he hadn't even bothered to wash my clothes. I would have demanded them back on the spot except that he seemed to have contaminated them with his pathetic version of me, and they were too filthy to touch anyway.

"Come on, David. Let's call your parents. Let's go down the hall and use the phone."

Abruptly his mood swung from tantrumming little boy lost to brutal, self-righteous rebel. He leaned his sweaty face into mine so that his three-week-old beard was almost tickling me. "My parents are NOT going to understand this. This is no duck pond. This is a revolution. Get it?"

"David, I just want to help," I said for the tenth time, each time wanting it less.

"Help the revolution," he smirked, and launched into a diatribe about the masses and the master class. I could tell he was faking it. This topic was an ironic kind of madness designed to divert me from whatever true paranoia he was secretly nurturing. The phrases he used sounded too familiar. They were parodies of arguments I had used with him just months ago.

I didn't scream, What gives you the right to impersonate me? What gives you the right to be my madness, my demise, personified? What gives you the right to literally empty out my life? Instead I said, "I'm only trying to help, David. Come on. I want you to call your parents now, or I will."

I was not gentle with him. I got a hold on the back of the Our Town T-shirt, right between his bony shoulder blades, and tugged him out of the corner. He walked down the hall in front of me with his chin straight up, like he was Susan Hayward in *I Want to Live* and I was his sympathetic executioner. I had to keep my hand gripped on the shirt so that it made a fist in his back and nudged him forward. At the same time, I kept him upright when his knees started to buckle and he lurched forward. I shoved a quarter into the slot and stood behind him while he made the call. I was consciously betraying him. They would almost certainly institutionalize him. They had done it before. Yet I stood behind him, listening to him whine and grovel and get incoherently enraged at his mother. Within a minute she demanded to talk to me. "Is he all right? Is he eating? Is he hallucinating? Is he taking his medication? How could you leave him alone for three weeks?"

"I'm sorry," I said, that excruciating phrase that is at best completely inadequate and at worst a lie. "I didn't know. I just found him like this."

We talked for a while, and it was clear that she wanted me to handle things. In her mind, I was his deviant girlfriend. Each of us wanted badly for the other to take care of David so we wouldn't have to do it ourselves. Each of us needed to believe that he was the other's responsibility. I tried to explain that I at least needed the phone bill paid, but that just gave her the moral high ground. How could I think about money at a time like this? How could I think only about myself?

"Now you listen to me, young lady. That's my son you're toying with. Do you understand me? I'll not have you abuse him any more." She talked as though a motherly tone of righteous indignation could solve everything.

I was no longer under control. "No, you listen. You listen to me, *old* lady. You are *not* my mother. I do not have to take this kind of bullshit from you. I am not related to you. I am barely a friend of your fucked-up son. You people are total fucking strangers to me. What happens to you doesn't matter to me. You have nothing to do with me. Nothing at all."

"You watch your language, Miss Fancy-pants. I will call your mother. I will tell her about this behaviour, and we'll see about that. Now you take that boy and you feed him, give him a bath and put him to bed. He doesn't need any more fun and games. He needs rest."

"You leave my mother out of this," I screamed into the phone, but it was impossible to leave her out. My mother was the empty space around me wherever I was. Not Wendy, not Mary-Jane, not Sarah, not Geoff and certainly not Mom herself had succeeded in adequately filling that space. How was it Mom was suddenly speaking to me through the voice of David's mother? I mumbled to myself, "You are not my mother," because I wanted to be convinced. I wanted the certainty of the little bird in the children's story who falls out of his nest and examines every object and animal he meets until he can say with certainty, "You are not my mother. I will find her. I will. I will."

David waited patiently in his inaccessible, personal hell. I didn't care what he was feeling. Probably, just the fact that, for as long as I was on the phone with his mother, he didn't have to face her or me with our binding failure, and shame provided him with some relief. When I finally hung up, long after communication ceased, David and I sat down on the floor together, and I cried like a kitten in a drowning bucket sliding down the well. David was already on the other side of sanity, but he was taking me along for the ride. I rolled around on the floor and called out, "I want my Mommy. Mommy, Mommy, I want to go home. Take me. Take me. Take me." I repeated it until it made sense. It was a Sunday, and that particular corridor of the university was empty except for us. The tiles felt clammy and cold through my clothes. The floor had just been washed and it struck me like a revelation that the scent of Pinesol was necessarily poisonous. The smell was everywhere.

David was watching me with apparent disgust. People in his family loathed public displays of self-indulgence. "Smarten up," he said. "You're acting like a baby."

Part of me wanted to stay, breathe in all that clean poison and die and get it over with, but something made me get up. I started to run. Who knows if David would have tried to follow me? He was too weak to keep up, and I felt a small triumph at shaking him so easily. I left him in the hallway outside the chess club with nothing but my clothes on his back. I hoped the Pinesol would take him quickly and painlessly.

SOME TIME HAS passed—a few days, and I have so far managed to keep from looking for David. Someone calls several times a day, maybe David, but I instantly hang up. Soon the phone will be disconnected. A warning letter from the phone company has already come. There is still very little in the apartment except the letters from Sarah, Mary-Jane and Wendy, and Sandrine's mysterious face.

The strangest part is not my feeling of my own absence here, but the absence of the past. If David is still alive, he is out there somewhere, still wearing my clothes, still being himself as the inevitable me. I want to wrest myself back from him, but just now I am afraid to face him. All my life, I have been running desperately and optimistically towards some better future place. I think of him out there somewhere, maybe sleeping on a bench in parc Lafontaine, holding a doggy bag with vinegar packets, napkins, toothpicks and my madness in store for me. I am here alone, in the stillness of these rooms, and it feels like one last reprieve from the complete loss of myself. When you cross that border into the world of madness, I don't know if you can ever fully come back. How complicated life is. Anyway, part of me would like to rush out and find him. I would grab the loot bag and shout "Mine! Mine! Mine!" to David and the ducks in the park and the other don't-wannabees that inhabit places like that.

"BUT NOT YET / you say extending the / time indefinitely by / your love until. . . ." Until the phone rings again for the twentieth time in the last hour, and I know it must be David again, shadowing me like Mr. Death on parking patrol. So, just to confound him, I answer the phone as if I'm a receptionist at a hair salon: "Good afternoon. How can I help you?"

"Lizzy?"

"Sarah?"

"I've been trying to get you all day. I called *The Mirror*

and they said you were back from Paris, but home sick. Are you okay? How was Paris? God, it's good to talk to you."

I could tell she had news. Sarah would never call long distance during the day without "news." It was like her to hear me out first; display a thorough interest in my life.

"Paris was amazing. Everyone there is French. I got a card for you of the Gargoyles, but I haven't sent it yet."

"Are you okay, Lizzy?"

"Yeah, just jet-lagged, I think. I haven't found my land-legs yet." It is a small miracle, I guess, but just the act of talking to her, talking to Sarah, my big sister, Sarah, the steady one, Sarah, the practical one, Sarah, the one who was always there just ahead of me, Sarah, who could out-run me, but could never get me off her trail; just the act of talking with her jerks me back from the abyss and into the world she's always grudgingly shared with me. She is too old to tell me to get lost or shrivel up like a slug. Instead, she wants to indulge me with her big-sisterly wisdom, and I let her.

I tell her about Mary-Jane's "lamb who strayed from the flock" attack. "Do you think she just saw me as one more soul to add to the roster?"

"Who cares? She was kind to you. She always liked you better than me. That should make you happy," she says, with her usual slight edginess.

I tell her about David, and we share a few moments of outrage together about the phone bill and the empty apartment.

"You sure know how to pick 'em," she says more than once. There is a silence wherein we both ponder the enormity of my bad judgement. Then Sarah gets practical and starts talking about scouting pawn shops, getting David some help and pleading for leniency with the phone company. We sort out my life and then go on to talking about Dad and Wendy's break-up, Karl's new teaching job, and the progress on the new house Sarah and Eric are fixing up. Sarah's "news," it turns out, is not a birth, death, marriage or illness, but just that Eric is coming through Montreal with his soccer team and hoping to have time to see me.

Off the phone, I toy with climbing back into the paranoia/paralysis mood, but I can't quite find it. Instead, I do what Sarah would do: make a list of priorities in my head: clean the bathroom, live, take a shower, live, go for a walk, live, call in to work and on and on.

Sooner or later we must come to the end of striving... but not yet.